"Tell me what to do," Hallie pleaded with her mother.

"You have to do what's best for you. Whatever you decide I'm behind you one hundred percent."

"But Dad—"

"He wants what's best for you, too, Hallie, and there's only one person who can answer that."

"But I don't know," Hallie wailed.

"Well then, you better think about it, because school starts in a few weeks, and if you're going to stay here, we have to register you, and we have to—"

"Maybe I should just go back."

"Don't take the easy way out, Hallie. The easy way is sometimes the hardest way in the long run. . . ."

CITY GIRL, COUNTRY GIRL

Marilyn Levy

FAWCETT JUNIPER • NEW YORK

RL1: $\dfrac{\text{VL 5 \& up}}{\text{IL 6 \& up}}$

A Fawcett Juniper Book
Published by Ballantine Books
Copyright © 1993 by Marilyn Levy

Library of Congress Catalog Card Number: 93-90088

ISBN 0-449-70424-6

Manufactured in the United States of America

First Edition: June 1993

I would like to thank two people for whose assistance I am most grateful. Cassie, who advised me on the story, and Genevieve Laycock–Wallis, who gave me permission to use her poem, *upon reaching puberty: a story for my daughter*.

Chapter One

It was eleven o'clock. The house was so quiet, Hallie could hear herself breathing. So quiet she could hear the kitchen clock ticking, the eucalyptus leaves brushing against her window, the music of the Santa Ana winds drifting across the roof. So quiet she could hear dogs, blocks away, howling at the moon, and small animals scampering across the patio. Cats maybe. Or mice. She wasn't afraid of mice like a lot of kids are. Maybe because she had had a pet mouse when she was younger. And maybe because of the story her mother used to read to her, her favorite bedtime story, "The City Mouse and the Country Mouse."

She wondered if she still had that old book. She was sure she'd seen it around the house somewhere. It had been her mother's back when her mother was a little girl. Her grandmother had read it to her mother, and her mother had read it to her. "Someday you can read this to your daughter," her mother had said. Little did Hallie suspect then that one day she would understand what life was like for each mouse—from personal experience.

The book never mentioned exactly where the city mouse and country mouse lived, but Hallie and her

1

mother always substituted Venice when it said "city" because that's where they lived. In Venice, California. And it was fun to think that the city mouse might have lived in their very own house. If she were reading the book now, she could substitute Maplewood, Oregon for the home of the country mouse.

Hallie sighed. The country mouse and the city mouse were like two sides of her.

For a moment she wondered if she should crawl out of bed and search for the book. Maybe it would help her make her decision.

A full moon lit up her room, and she glanced at the clock on the table beside her bed. *In an hour it would be tomorrow*. And tomorrow was the day she had promised she would tell her mother what she had decided to do.

Instead of getting out of bed, Hallie drew the sheet up to her chin, then continued pulling on it until it covered her face and her head. Maybe she could just disappear. That way she wouldn't have to think about IT anymore. She wouldn't have to think about anything.

She lay under the sheet for a long time, trying not to think. It didn't work. She couldn't keep her mind quiet. Her thoughts kept leaping around, jumping from one subject to the next. She thought about everything except the one thing on which she should have been concentrating.

She thought about her dog, Fuzzy. She thought about her baby sister, Molly. She thought about the new clothes she had bought when she and her mother went shopping. She thought about the way Frank looked when he jogged down the street, which made her think of Fuzzy again, which made her think of Oregon, which made her think of her father, which made her think of her decision, which made her groan out loud and bury herself even more deeply under the sheet. Maybe if she could just fall asleep, the answer would come to her in her dreams, and she would wake up in the morning and know exactly what to do.

She put her hands down at her sides and lay perfectly still. But it didn't help. She couldn't sleep. She was wide awake. Slowly, she removed the sheet from her head, then peeled it away from her body. She sighed and rolled out of bed. There was only one thing to do: look for "The City Mouse and the Country Mouse."

She scanned the shelves of her bookcase, sure she wouldn't find it, but hoping by some miracle it would be there anyway. It wasn't. She opened all the drawers in her dresser and searched through them, knowing there was no way it was there. She lifted her quilt and looked under her bed. She found her tennis racket, the sweater she'd misplaced last week, and the lipstick she wasn't supposed to wear. But no book.

She sat down at her desk and stared at the blank piece of paper sitting on top of it. Then she got out a ruler and a pencil and began making columns before she consciously realized what she was doing.

Almost against her will, she began the long process she'd been putting off. Until two weeks ago, she'd had a perfectly happy summer. Well—not exactly perfect. And not entirely happy. But that was a different story. Or maybe it wasn't. She started to panic. Instead of making things clearer, she was confusing herself even more.

She began again. Until two weeks ago, she'd thought she had come back to spend only the summer with her mother. She had planned on returning to Oregon right before school started. Then her mother had put this thought into her head. Not maliciously, or anything. And to be honest, it wasn't exactly a thought. It was more like the germ of a thought. Her mother had simply said, "Hallie, you've been in a really bad mood for the past few days. What's bothering you?"

As soon as her mother pointed out that she was in a bad mood, Hallie denied it, told her mother *she* was the one in a bad mood and ran to her bedroom.

Then she was stuck. The TV was in the living room. The book she was reading was in the kitchen, and she remembered that she'd kicked off her ballet slippers and left them next to her mother's bed. But even if she had them, they wouldn't do her any good. The CD player was in the living room next to the television set, so she couldn't play any music, anyway. She plopped down on her bed and continued sulking.

But at the back of her mind—way back in a distant, crowded corner—unbidden thoughts kept blowing toward her like the flecks of dust you can see when sunlight streams in through a window. You know they're there, but you can't really capture them.

And then it happened. It was almost as if a gust of wind swept the thoughts out of the corner of her mind and right before her eyes. They stood before her in bold letters. I DON'T HAVE TO GO BACK TO OREGON. I CAN STAY HERE IN CALIFORNIA.

She opened her bedroom door as quietly as she could and listened to the sounds of the house. Her mother was in the kitchen. That was a good sign. She was singing to herself. That was an even better sign. If she were angry, she'd be in her studio trying to paint Ereshkigal, a dark female goddess who lived in the underworld, according to an ancient myth. Her mother said Ereshkigal haunted her and made her doubt herself.

Hallie walked into the kitchen and opened the refrigerator.

"I just cut up some watermelon. Want some?" Michelle asked as she arranged the red wedges on a platter.

Michelle wasn't her mother's given name, of course. That was Ann. But her mother had changed her name two years ago, after she got divorced. "I need to feel more glamorous," she had said to Hallie.

Hallie picked up a slice of watermelon and stuck it in her mouth. She liked the coolness against her tongue and the sweet flavor. "What if I don't go back to Oregon?" she asked her mother, without looking at her.

Her mother didn't answer her. Hallie didn't know if she should repeat the question, or assume that no answer meant her mother wasn't thrilled with the idea of her staying in California.

She heard Frank's Land-Rover in the driveway and decided she knew which it was. She picked up another piece of watermelon and headed for her room.

"Hallie," her mother called to her. "There's nothing I'd like better than for you to stay here and go to school. But I think you ought to weigh this carefully. You're starting ninth grade. That's high school. Once you make a commitment, it won't be easy to keep changing schools."

"Does that mean I should stay, or I shouldn't?"

"It means that it's up to you."

"Tell me what to do."

"You have to do what's best for you. Whatever you decide, I'm behind you one hundred percent."

"But Dad—"

"He wants what's best for you, too, Hallie, and there's only one person who can answer that."

"But I don't know," Hallie wailed.

"Well then, you better think about it, because school starts in a few weeks, and if you're going to stay here, we have to register you, and we have to—"

"Maybe I should just go back."

"Don't take the easy way out, Hallie. The easy way is sometimes the hardest way in the long run."

"I'm staying," Hallie said. But before the words were out of her mouth, she heard the front door slam, and she regretted them. "No. I'm going back."

"Why don't you list all the positive things you can think of about Venice," her mother suggested. "Then list all the negatives. Do the same thing for Maplewood. That might help you make your decision."

"I don't think so. Either I'm going, or I'm staying," Hallie said. The last thing she wanted to do was organize her thoughts and write them out like a school assignment.

"Up to you," her mother said, as Frank swept into the kitchen carrying a huge bouquet of flowers.

"My favorite girls," he said, first kissing Hallie, then her mother.

"Women," her mother said. "Not girls."

"Hallie's too young to be a woman."

"She's a young woman."

"When do girls become young women? And when do young women become old ladies?"

"Girls become young women when they get their periods," her mother said.

Hallie could feel the heat rising up in her face. Why did her mother have to embarrass her like that? Why did she have to tell Frank everything! He wasn't her father.

"And women never, never, never become old ladies. At least this woman doesn't plan to."

Frank laughed and plucked a red carnation out of the bouquet. He put it in his mouth, then started doing a flamenco dance, clicking his heels and jumping in the air. If any of Hallie's friends had walked into the house at that moment, she would have been mortified. Frank was fun, but sometimes he got a little carried away. Contractors were supposed to be solid, dependable people, just like the houses they built. But Frank somehow refused to recognize that. He wore wild Hawaiian shirts and red high tops with no socks. It made Hallie crazy. Not all the time. But certainly when her father was in town.

Her father thought that men should look like men— and act like them, too. He thought that real warriors didn't go out into the woods, beat on drums, and read poetry. They went to snag dinner and bring it home.

Hallie looked at Frank. Her father had a point.

"So what about that list, Hallie?" her mother asked.

"What list?" Hallie asked, pretending she'd forgotten.

Michelle walked over to Frank and took the carnation out of his mouth.

"Hallie's thinking about going to school here next year," her mother said to Frank.

Frank whirled around and looked at Hallie.

"Great," he said a little too quickly. "That's great."

Chapter Two

When Hallie finished drawing the columns, she glanced at the clock. *It was now eleven-fifteen.* Quickly she wrote "MAPLEWOOD" in large letters at the top of the page. At the head of the first column she wrote pluses. At the top of the second column she wrote minuses.

MAPLEWOOD	
Pluses	Minuses

She sat looking at the sheet for a long time, but she couldn't think of anything to put in either column. Her mind was totally blank. She took out a second sheet of paper and wrote "VENICE" at the top of the page, and then proceeded to draw the columns and write pluses and minuses.

She put her pencil down. It was no use. She started to crush the paper and toss it into the wastepaper bas-

ket, but as she stared down at the lines, they seemed to
form into the old farmhouse in Oregon. She smoothed
out the paper, hesitated for a moment, then wrote
"farmhouse" under pluses. She paused, looked at what
she had written, and without erasing it, wrote "farmhouse" under the minus column as well.

Before last year, she had never even been on a farm.
The closest she had come to rolling hills of grass was
at the park, or at the houses of a few of her old friends.
Her house—the one she was living in now—was small.
Not counting her mother's studio, which was in a separate building behind the house, they had two bedrooms, one bathroom, a living room, and a big kitchen.

While she was gone, her mother had met Frank and
married him, just like that, before she had even gotten to
know him. And Frank had built a wooden deck onto the
side of the house and the studio for Michelle. Little by
little he was transforming the house. Adding another bathroom, enlarging the living room. But with each addition,
something was also subtracted. More than one thing, maybe. The obvious thing was that now there was no grass at
all. Just house, which was why Fuzzy was still in Oregon.

Next to "farmhouse," Hallie listed her caramel-colored
springer spaniel. She missed Fuzzy. She felt like playing
with him. She felt like scratching his stomach and tickling
the white vest of hair covering it. She felt like tugging at the
fuzz under his chin, throwing him a ball and watching him
chase after it. Most of all she felt like hugging him close to
her and whispering to him, asking him where he wanted to
live. But even sitting here, hundreds of miles away, she
knew what his answer would be. Where would any dog
rather be? Confined to a house and two inches of grass,

barely larger than her mother's sketch pad, or running around acres and acres of wooded land?

After her father and mother got divorced, they remained on speaking terms, for her sake probably. Most of the time they managed at least to appear to be friendly, and Hallie was grateful for that, though she couldn't help wondering exactly why they had split up. Before the divorce, sometimes when they thought she was asleep, she could hear them arguing. Her father would say that her mother talked too much, monopolized conversations, and embarrassed him at parties, especially when she had a few drinks. Her mother would cry and say that her father was cold and insensitive, that he didn't appreciate her and always put her down.

But the next morning, they would talk to each other as usual, and Hallie would wonder if she had dreamed it all. By the time breakfast was over, everything was totally back to normal, and she would forget about what she had heard the night before.

Then one day everything got really quiet. There was no more whispering, no more crying, no more talking at all. And her father moved his things out of the house and into a loft in downtown Los Angeles.

Her mother cried a whole lot for a while, then she started painting like crazy. She seemed pretty happy, and though Hallie hated the whole idea of her parents being divorced, in reality it wasn't all that bad.

One week she would stay with her father, and he would drive her to school every morning and pick her up every afternoon. And the next week she stayed at home with her mother.

One week while she was at home, Jane moved into the

loft. She'd met Jane a few times, but she hadn't really given her much thought, so it sort of shocked her. But her father acted as if it was the most natural thing in the world. And pretty soon, Hallie took this arrangement in stride, too. The only thing was that Jane seemed to take up so much space. She was big. Not fat, but big. Over six feet tall. And she was totally different from her mother. Her mother was tiny. Only five feet tall. She was very delicate-looking, with her short blond hair and big green eyes. Hallie was already taller than her mother, and thinner. She was built like her dad, tall and slender. And she looked like him, too. They both had dark wavy hair and high foreheads. But she had her mother's green eyes.

It was right after the Christmas program at Hallie's school that her father told her he and Jane were getting married. They'd been dropping hints, so she expected she would have to deal with that sooner or later, and she wasn't all that surprised. But she was blown over by his next two announcements. Jane was going to have a baby. And— and they were moving to Oregon in June.

Hallie felt the blood drain out of her face and her knees go weak. She could live without Jane—gladly—but she and her father had a special relationship. She loved him a lot. She depended on him. She wasn't even sure where Oregon was. And when she learned it was hundreds of miles away, she burst into tears.

"You'll spend all your vacations with us," her father said. "It'll be wonderful. You'll love Oregon."

She hated his saying "us" instead of "me." She didn't want to go to Oregon to spend time with Jane. It was probably Jane's fault they were moving there in the first place. She'd somehow talked her father into it. Cast a spell over him, or something. At least that's what her mother had jokingly suggested.

Hallie decided not to make an issue out of the "we" business since it wouldn't do much good. But still she was upset. "I'm going to ballet camp in Colorado this summer," she said. "Don't you remember?"

"That will give us time to set up. Get everything ready for you when you visit in July," her father said enthusiastically.

Hallie wondered if he was only pretending to be enthusiastic about her coming. It seemed like one day her father was in her life, and the next day he was gone. It was as if he was gradually leaving her behind. First he had moved out of the house. Now he was moving out of the state. He had a new wife, and pretty soon he would have a new baby. He would have a whole new family. Where would that put her?

Hallie tried to forget about it while she was at camp. And she could, as long as she was dancing. But at night, after lights out, she kept trying to figure out how everything had gotten so mixed up right under her nose, without her ever realizing what was going on.

Hallie and her mother made the trip to Oregon in three days, staying overnight in motels on the coast along the way. They had brought a bunch of tapes, and they sang and told stories. But there were also long periods of silence, and as they drove along the barren roads, through the redwood forests, angling around mountains high above the roaring ocean, she wondered what it was going to be like in this new place. Even before they left California, they seemed to be running out of civilization. The towns got further and further apart. And they got smaller and smaller. But there was something beautiful about the space and the quiet.

Hallie and her mother stopped at a seaside restaurant in Mendocino. The restaurant was little more than a shack, so they ordered crab sandwiches to go, and as they sat eating on the pier overlooking the Pacific Ocean, Hallie almost wished this was Oregon.

"Stand over there, so I can take your picture," her mother said after they had finished lunch and licked their fingers clean.

She posed, standing next to a fishing boat. The sun was warm on her face, but not too hot. The breeze played with her hair. She smiled at her mother. She heard the shutter click, then she danced away. This was a great vacation. For a moment Hallie forgot why she was there and where she was headed.

"I got the sea gulls swooping in on the bit of crab that fell out of your sandwich," her mother said as she focused on Hallie again.

Hallie had never considered herself stingy, and she probably would have offered some of her sandwich to the birds anyway, if she had thought of it. But she suddenly felt greedy. She didn't want to share her crabmeat with anyone or anything. She wanted it all to herself. Every last bit.

If she had known, at that moment, that she would wind up staying in Oregon for the whole school year instead of a month, she probably would have ordered another sandwich. But then again, if she had known she was going to do that, she would have been much too nervous to eat it.

Chapter Three

As soon as her mother pulled into the long driveway, her father raced out of the house and met them halfway. Her mother stopped the car, and Hallie opened the door and rushed over to her father. Fuzzy, feeling free after his long hours of confinement in the back seat, leapt out and ran around in circles before he sped off to a distant tree.

Hallie was so happy to see her father, she barely noticed her mother's hand rapidly twirling a lock of hair, indulging in an old nervous habit she thought she'd finally broken last year.

"Come on, I'll show you around," her father said.

"Come on, Mom."

"Maybe I better check into the motel—"

"You have plenty of time for that. Maplewood's not exactly a tourist attraction," her father said, and he smiled at her mother for the first time in a long while. "They'll hold your room."

Her mother, who had gotten out of the car and was now standing beside the open door, hesitated for a moment.

"Come on, Ann. I can't give you a complete tour of

the property because I'm baby-sitting, and Molly's asleep, but I can show you the house.''

"I'd like that," her mother said. She got back into the car and drove to the house while Hallie and her father walked up the driveway together.

The house wasn't anything like she had expected. Though her father had sent her photographs of the farm and the house and sketches of what they would like to do with it, the actual place itself was a disappointment. It was big. That was true. But the glossy pictures had made everything look shiny, almost new.

The house in the photographs had a silvery sheen, as if it had been welded together with quarters, promising a prosperity that the real house had probably never enjoyed. Even when it was new. It wasn't silver at all. It was gray. And badly in need of a paint job. It almost seemed as if her father had substituted a movie set for the real thing. Or had airbrushed out all the blemishes, the way photographers do in fashion photographs, so the women look perfect.

Hallie sneaked a look at her father, but he didn't seem to notice that anything was wrong with the place. He was obviously in love with the old farmhouse, warts and all.

The inside of the house was less disconcerting—at least at first glance. The old wood floors had been refinished and the wide pine planks had a warm, welcoming glow. But the furniture from her father's former apartment looked out of place, though she couldn't tell exactly why. Maybe black leather and an old potbellied stove didn't go together. Whatever it was, something seemed off.

"The leather stuff will eventually go in my office,"

her father said, as if he had read her mind. "But we haven't finished working on that yet."

From what Hallie could see, they hadn't begun to work on most of the house yet. The kitchen was big, bigger than the kitchen at home, but it, too, was old-fashioned, with an old stove you had to light with a match and a white porcelain sink of which her father was very proud, though for the life of her Hallie couldn't figure out why. It was just a sink. Not a very large one at that. And it had brownish stains running through it.

The most old-fashioned thing, though, was the bathroom. The little black and white tiles of the floor, the kind you find in creepy run-down houses, was another clue that this house was really, really old. A lot older than her father and mother. But the thing that knocked her out was the toilet. It didn't have a handle. There was a box on the wall above the toilet with a chain hanging from it, and *you had to pull the chain to flush the toilet*. This was one step up from an outhouse.

"Let's take a peek in Molly's room," her father whispered as they walked down the hallway.

He opened the door slowly, and they stuck their heads into a room which looked as if it belonged in another house. Everything was so white and so clean, Hallie was dazzled. Even the wood floors were painted a glossy white. And miniature winged animals in every shape and color danced across a lower wall panel circling the room.

"It looks like a magical zoo," her mother said.

"Look up," her father whispered.

There were white clouds and stars and a silver moon painted on the high ceiling, which was light blue.

Hallie swallowed hard and tiptoed further into the

room. It was so beautiful, but for some reason she felt like crying. "I wish I could hold her," she whispered, as she blinked back her tears and peered at Molly, sound asleep in her white lacquered crib.

"You'll have plenty of time for that," her father said, and he put his finger over his lips and motioned toward the door.

"Where's my room?" Hallie asked when they were back in the hallway.

"It's not really finished yet," her father said. "We thought we'd get you to help us fix it up."

He stopped in front of an open door and stepped aside so she could walk in.

There was a single bed with a maple wood headboard and an old quilt covering it. The only other piece of furniture in the room was a matching five-drawer chest.

"The furniture came with the house," her father said enthusiastically. "Must be about a hundred years old."

"Looks like it," Hallie said under her breath.

"And the quilt was a real find. We bought it from an old couple down the road who were moving in with one of their children. Said it had been in the family for three generations, but their daughter didn't want it. They were glad it was going to someone who would appreciate it. Don't you love it, Hallie?"

"Yeah," Hallie said, and she thought of her bedroom at home with its white down quilt and white pillow shams, and all the stuffed animals sitting on it.

"I think I'll stay at the motel with Mom tonight," she said, begging her mother with her eyes to say that was okay.

"But we haven't seen you for almost two months," her father protested.

"You'll have her for the rest of the summer," her mother said. "Let me have her for one more night."

"Jane will be disappointed. She's been—"

"I'll drop her off first thing in the morning."

"Tell Jane I'm sorry I missed her. I'll see her tomorrow," Hallie said, as they walked down the creaking steps to the outer hallway.

"I'm really disappointed," her father said. Grudgingly, he opened the front door for them.

Hallie lowered her eyes. "Maybe I should—"

"We'll be back at nine in the morning," her mother said. "I want to get an early start."

"Around here that's a late start," her father countered.

Hallie knew he was trying to keep the annoyance out of his voice, but he hadn't quite managed it.

"Well, whatever. We'll be here around nine."

The only time Hallie ever heard her mother use that tone of voice was with her father. She always knew when her mother was talking to her father on the phone. Not so much because of the words she said, but because of the way she said them. Usually, her voice was soft, almost musical, but when she talked to her father it was as if the words got caught in her throat, and she had to spit them out, or lose them.

"We'll show you around the property tomorrow," her father promised.

Hallie picked Fuzzy up and carried him back to the car.

Her father stood in the doorway and waved as her mother backed the car up and turned around.

Hallie waved back. "Bye," she said softly, almost mouthing the words.

Her mother glanced at her, but she didn't say anything. Hallie didn't say anything either.

"Damn, forgot to ask him for directions to the motel," her mother said.

She started heading toward the house again, then she looked over at Hallie leaning against the window and changed her mind.

"Never mind. We'll find it."

Chapter Four

It wasn't the kind of farm you see in movies, or the kind you read about in books. At least it wasn't the kind of farm Hallie had expected it to be. Except for the patch of land that had been cleared by the house, nothing had grown there for many years. While it was true that there were acres and acres of land, low prickly blackberry bushes and briers covered most of it, camouflaging what was once verdant earth. Hallie was thinking this as she sat eating her first dinner at the farm.

"We've cleared out almost half an acre," Jane said proudly. "These tomatoes, the lettuce, the corn are all from our garden. So are the chives and parsley, the potatoes."

"How come you don't keep a cow like they do on real farms, so you can grow your own milk, too?" Hallie asked.

Her father frowned at her for a moment, as if he were trying to decide whether or not Hallie was being sarcastic. If he had called her on it, she wouldn't have been able to deny it. The words had just tumbled out of her mouth of their own volition, as if they had come from some other being, some angel or demon. Perhaps Eresh-kigal had made her do it.

"Maybe we will buy a cow," her father said, study-ing Hallie's face for a clue to her state of mind.

Hallie stared at her food, shutting down any emotion that might have unwittingly crept into her end of the conversation.

"Or maybe even a horse. But we'll have to clean out the barn first," her father said lightheartedly.

Hallie was relieved.

"Project number three hundred and six. Right now it looks as if no one has touched it for twenty years."

"Think Mom'll call tonight?" Hallie asked.

Her father and Jane exchanged glances. "She said she'd check in," her father said.

"Maybe you and your dad can go fishing tomorrow," Jane said. "There's a great stream not far from here— near where I grew up. My mom and dad still live there."

Hallie looked across the table at Jane; she knew she had been right about why her father had suddenly de-cided to leave Los Angeles and move to Oregon. It wasn't just because the air was better and life was slower, easier, safer—like he said. It was because of Jane. She didn't know what Jane had said or done to make him believe that living in the country was so won-derful, but at least she understood why he had just picked up and left her. He had a choice, and he had made it.

"I didn't know you liked to fish, Dad."

"Neither did I. Jane showed me how."

"You sure couldn't fish off the Venice pier," Jane said, and she laughed.

"That's not true," Hallie said. "I've seen people fishing there."

"Mexicans."

"So?"

"The ocean's polluted along the coast. I wouldn't even swim in it, let alone eat anything caught in those waters."

"In Oregon people respect the environment," her father explained. "Up here, people don't take natural resources for granted."

"My mom recycles bottles, cans, plastic—everything," Hallie said. "She has a fit if I forget and toss one Coke can in the garbage."

"Well, it's nice to know your mom's obsessing on something besides her poetry," her father said, and he chuckled and winked at Hallie.

But Hallie didn't smile. Her father's remark stung her. Even when they were living together and arguing a lot, he'd never said anything negative about her directly to Hallie, and her mother had never said anything negative about him. It was as if he'd broken an unwritten law, and it upset her, especially since her mother wasn't there to defend herself. "She's not writing poetry any more," Hallie said. "She's painting."

"Well, that's nice," her father said.

Hallie thought she noticed a little smirk flicker across his face.

"As long as she enjoys it," he added.

"Dad," Hallie cried. "She's really good. Everyone says so. She was even invited to show her work in a gallery."

Hallie could feel her face getting hot. It wasn't exactly that her father's last comment was negative. It was the way he'd said it. It was criticism with a big, round, yellow smiley face, the kind Ms. Crandle put at the bottom of her papers to soften all the negative comments she'd made in red ink.

"Hey, I think your mom's very talented," her father said quickly. "And she has excellent taste. She edits all my books, doesn't she?"

"Isn't Jane going to edit them now?" Hallie asked.

Her father laughed softly. "Jane has other virtues."

"And editing books isn't one of them," Jane said, winking at her father.

Hallie suddenly felt embarrassed, as if she were eavesdropping on a private moment.

But the moment passed and was lost somewhere in time, perhaps to be recaptured some day, in one way or another, by Hallie, or her father, or Jane, any one of them, or none of them at all.

After dinner, they all cleared the table. Just as Jane filled the sink to wash the dishes, Molly let out a shriek.

"Saved by the call of nurture," Jane said, looking down at the wet streak which suddenly appeared on her shirt.

"Want to come up and keep me company while I feed her?"

"What about the dishes?" Hallie asked.

Surprisingly, her father volunteered to do them, something he'd never done at home, and Hallie followed Jane up the stairs.

As Hallie stood in the doorway watching, Jane bent down and cooed over the baby as she lifted her out of the crib. She put her down on the changing table and removed her white cloth diaper, talking to Molly and smiling at her the whole time, as if she had forgotten Hallie's presence.

Then she settled into a rocking chair, unbuttoned her blue work shirt and held Molly to her swollen breast.

Hallie was embarrassed by the sight of the gigantic breast and remembered the day her mother had referred to Jane as a cow. Or perhaps it was one of her mother's friends who had said that. She didn't remember exactly. But whoever had said it was right, she thought. At this moment, Jane looked like a cow being milked.

Why had she asked Hallie to come upstairs with her? And why had Hallie followed her up like a puppy? What was she supposed to do? Just stand there and watch Jane feed the baby as if she were viewing some sports event?

Hallie was about to turn away and walk back down the stairs when Jane looked up at her.

"Isn't she the most beautiful baby you've ever seen?"

"Yeah, I guess so," Hallie said grudgingly.

"She's my little doll."

Hallie cocked her head to the side and studied Jane for a moment. She was big-boned, that was true, but Hallie realized for the first time how young she was, much younger than her father and mother, who had had Hallie when they were in their thirties.

Jane's long, tapered fingers were twice the size of her mother's dainty hands, but there was something almost romantic about them, and her long, white legs sticking out from her faded cutoff jeans were covered with scratches and bruises, just like a kid's.

"I can't believe she's mine," Jane said, wrinkling her nose so that the freckles fused, making one large red mark.

As if to remind her she was a real baby and not a doll, Molly lost the nipple for a moment and lurched sideways, letting out a short cry. Then she latched onto the breast again, heaved a deep sigh, and, content that all was right in her little world, went back to her feeding.

Hallie looked away. She flexed her right leg and stretched it out in front of her. She arched her foot and pointed her toe, as if she were getting into position to begin practicing her dance steps. Instead, she ran her toe back and forth across the polished white floor, making arcs in front of her left foot.

Chapter Five

By the end of the first week in Oregon, Hallie felt numb. It wasn't as if things were so bad that she couldn't stand it, it was more that she had lost her bearings.

Hallie had been given responsibilities around the house immediately, which was all right with her, since there was nothing else to do, and it relieved the boredom—and the uncomfortable feeling she had that she was marooned on an island with three strangers with whom she didn't even share a common language. Oh, they all spoke English, of course. It wasn't that. It was something deeper than that. And she couldn't even narcotize herself by overdosing on TV.

Maplewood, Oregon received only one television station, and even that didn't come in very well. She noticed a big satellite dish in someone's yard when she went for a walk, and she had mentioned it to her father when she got home. But he insisted one station was enough. Too much. He certainly wasn't going to ruin his pristine property by installing ugly technology.

So she had had time, lots of time, with nothing to do but think. And she concluded that her mother was wrong when she quoted some ancient philosopher named Socrates, who had said, ''The life which is

unexamined is not worth living.'' It was the examined
life that gave you problems. Once you started thinking
too much, things suddenly seemed a lot worse than they
really were. Or maybe they had been, but she hadn't
known it. So which was better, obsessing over each
little conflict or moment of unhappiness, or moving on?

Moving on, she decided. But when she tried to lift
her feet, she found them tied together, so to speak. She
had put on her ballet slippers a few times, but there
wasn't really enough space to practice in her bedroom,
and she felt uncomfortable leaping across the living
room floor in front of the open windows, even though
her father assured her their nearest neighbors were a
mile away.

So she didn't mind cleaning up after breakfast, or
walking Molly in her stroller for an hour every day so
she could get some fresh air, or helping clear the brush
on Saturday, which Jane explained was their weekly ritual. In fact, it was sort of fun working all together, even
though she wound up with the same scratches and
bruises Jane had all over her legs. And when they were
finished, you couldn't even tell they'd really done anything. They hadn't made a dent. But the work, more
than anything else, cleared her head a little and made
her feel less numb. Maybe because all her energy went
into using her body and not her brain—what was left
of it.

The rest of the time she spent lying on her bed, le-
thargically turning pages in a book she read and re-read
without remembering the main character's name from
one day to the next, let alone the plot.

Or she found herself just roaming aimlessly around
the house and the land adjacent to it. She'd walk past

the old barn without really seeing it and circle the property a few times, or wander down to a stream, take off her tennis shoes and socks, and wade in it for a while until she would suddenly realize her feet were numb with cold. But she didn't really take notice of anything. The world around her entered her consciousness only peripherally, and she vaguely wondered what she would do for the next three weeks.

Occasionally, she played with Fuzzy, throwing him a stick and waiting for him to retrieve it. But Fuzzy was so busy exploring the land and staking out his territory that he barely ran up to nuzzle her anymore.

Jane said it was better for dogs to be outside all the time. At first, Hallie had balked at the idea, insisting that Fuzzy wasn't an outside dog. He always slept in her bedroom, right beside her bed. Then one day she realized Fuzzy had not only adjusted to his new life a lot better than she had, he actually loved the freedom of the wide open space. But instead of making her feel better, for some reason, it felt like another loss.

It was nearly midnight, and Hallie was no closer to making her decision. In a sense, she was even farther away from it. She nervously chewed the eraser on the end of her pencil. Until now, she hadn't even realized how upset she had been that first week in Oregon. Until now, she hadn't even remembered. Or maybe she hadn't really felt it. Maybe she had been too numb—too scared to feel. Scared of what, she wondered? Of her father? Of Jane? Of being away from home? She'd been at dance camp for three weeks, and she wasn't scared there. She didn't know what she was afraid of. But she did know that if there had been no second and third week in Oregon, she wouldn't have a problem deciding what to do now, because she wouldn't have stayed there one minute longer than she had to. Even if that meant not being with her father.

Sitting in her bedroom in Venice, however, some things suddenly became clearer, and she realized that, even though she and her father hadn't understood how unhappy she was that first week, Jane must have known. Maybe because Jane was closer to her age, and she remembered how kids felt.

It was actually because of Jane that she had met Kate Evans.

And after she met Kate, Hallie began to look at the things around her through Kate's eyes. She saw that the barn was more than an old run-down building with holes in the roof. The last paint job had long ago peeled away, that was true, but the wood was left with a weather-beaten look the color of ash, and was almost smooth to the touch.

Everything looked different to Hallie after that first week. Even Molly looked different. Hallie sometimes found herself leaning over the baby's crib, hoping she'd wake up, so she could play with her.

Until tonight, she had thought that she and Kate had met accidentally. But now she wasn't so sure. Jane hadn't actually arranged for them to meet, but one night she had driven into town for something, and the next night she had suggested they drive to town for ice cream after dinner.

Hallie smiled remembering how shy she felt when she and Jane and her father, carrying Molly in his arms, walked into Ben & Jerry's.

* * *

The store was packed with kids. Big kids, little kids, teenagers. It was obviously the place to hang out, and everyone seemed to know everyone else. Everybody except Hallie and her little group. She tried to hide behind Jane so she wouldn't be so conspicuous. It was embarrassing being the only kid with parents, except for the kids who were fourth graders or under.

Then Jane, her voice booming so loudly everyone could hear her, asked Hallie what she wanted to order.

"Whatever," Hallie mumbled. "I don't care."

And she didn't. All she cared about was getting out of there as quickly as possible. She was sure everyone was looking at them, thinking they were really weird.

She was staring down at the floor as Jane and her father ordered, so she didn't notice the freckle-faced girl break away from her group of friends and walk over to them. She didn't even look up when she heard the girl say, "Ohhhh, how cute. What's her name?" Because, for a moment, Hallie felt the blood drain out of her face, and she went into shock. She thought the girl was talking about her. It wasn't until she heard her father say, "Molly," that Hallie realized the girl was looking at the baby.

So she would put Kate, with her deep, crackling voice that sometimes sounded like a stick breaking in two, in the plus column. There was no question about that. Plus. Plus. The minute she had had the courage to look up at Kate that night in Ben & Jerry's, she saw the strange mixture of sophistication and innocence on her face, and she knew she was standing in front of somebody very powerful.

"I'm Kate Evans," Kate said to Jane and her father,

without a trace of embarrassment or shyness. "You guys are new in town, huh?"

"Moved in two months ago," her father said.

"Seen you guys around. You bought the old Miller place, huh?"

"Right," Jane said.

"Like it here?"

"Love it," her father said.

"Yeah, all the people from L.A. say that, but they usually don't stick around for too long," Kate said, and she laughed good-naturedly. "Too borrrrrring." She laughed again. Easily and without a trace of guile or resentment. Then she suddenly turned to Hallie. "Haven't seen you before. Been away at camp, or something?"

"Me?" Hallie gulped.

"No, the baby," Kate said, and she giggled unexpectedly.

That kind of answer ordinarily made Hallie feel like finding the nearest hole and crawling into it. But for some reason this time she swallowed hard and looked right at Kate.

"Well, Molly spent the summer painting the house. I was at dance camp," Hallie said, surprising herself.

Kate broke into laughter, as if she enjoyed being the butt of Hallie's joke, and Hallie realized that teasing was Kate's way of being friendly.

"Yeah, and who are you?" she asked, pretending to be tough.

"Hallie."

"What grade you in?"

"Going into eighth."

"Me too. We'll be in the same classes. There's only one eighth grade at school."

"But—"

"Kate," some of the kids across the room yelled. "Come on."

"My dad's here," one of the other kids yelled.

"I'm not—"

"I gotta go," Kate said, before Hallie could tell her she wouldn't be going to school here in the fall. She was only in Maplewood for the rest of the summer.

When she was at the door, Kate turned back to her. "I'll ride over to see you some day. I live just down the road."

"Okay," Hallie said, but Kate didn't hear her. She was already out the door.

Chapter Six

It was quiet. Her father was in his half-finished office at the back of the house, pounding away at his word processor, and Jane had driven into Eugene with Molly for Molly's monthly checkup. She had invited Hallie to come along, but Hallie had declined. It was an hour's ride there and another hour back. And though she was beginning to feel more comfortable with Jane, Hallie didn't want to be trapped in a car with her for two hours straight. In the silence of a car, people were tempted to ask too many questions, and other people were sometimes tempted to answer them.

So Hallie just sat on her bed staring out the window without really seeing anything. Someone walking into the room might have surmised that she was lost in her thoughts. But they would have been wrong. She was simply lost. She wasn't thinking about anything at all. At least she wasn't consciously thinking.

She was startled when she heard her name being called. At first she thought she had imagined hearing it, then she heard it again. She swung her legs over the side of the bed and walked to the window so she could see more than just the tops of trees.

Below her window, sitting on a horse, was Kate Evans.

They stared at each other for a moment. Then Kate cupped her hands to her mouth and shouted, "You coming, or not?"

"I'm coming," Hallie shouted back, and she ran down the steps and out the front door before she had time to wonder where it was they were going.

"Hi," Hallie said, shielding her eyes from the sun as she looked up at Kate.

"Thought maybe you forgot," Kate said.

"But you didn't tell me—" Hallie began to protest.

"Doesn't matter," Kate said impatiently. "We have plenty of time."

Time for what, Hallie wondered. She gingerly put her hand on the horse's mane. She'd never seen a horse up close before.

"His name is Mercury."

"Mercury?"

"Yeah—like the god in Roman mythology. He's a stallion."

Hallie blushed. "I can see that," she mumbled.

"Mercury was the god of travel, the messenger," Kate said.

"Who named him?"

"I did. He's my horse. My dad bought him for himself, but the two of us fell in love at first sight. Didn't we, boy?" Kate stroked Mercury's mane.

Hallie could understand immediately why Kate and the horse had fallen in love. They looked as though they were related. They had the same coloring. Reddish. Both Kate and Mercury had copper-colored hair, and even Kate's arms and legs were reddish in color. If you squinted your eyes, it was sometimes hard to tell the rider from the horse though it was evident to Hallie that both rider and horse were beautiful specimens.

Still, beauty can sometimes be frightening, and there was something a little scary about the horse, so when he reared slightly and whinnied, Hallie jumped.

Simultaneously, Kate threw back her head, arched her back, and laughed. And Hallie noted once again how much alike the horse and rider were.

Kate leaned down close to the horse's ear, so that the top of her body lay across his neck. She whispered something to him. Then she patted Mercury's side. As if he had heard her and was responding, he tapped his hoof twice and whinnied once again.

Kate straightened up. "Get on," she said to Hallie.

Hallie stood there looking at both the horse and the girl. How, she wondered, did one go about getting on? She'd seen people put their feet in stirrups and jump onto horses in movies, but she had no idea how they did it. While they made it look natural, even easy, in real life it seemed impossible. Even if she could figure out how to put her foot in the stirrup, and which foot went where, the horse's back still seemed much too far from the ground for her.

She felt like crying. Her first major test with a new friend, and she'd failed miserably. Automatically, she began backing away, but before she had moved more than a few inches, Kate jumped off the horse and landed on the ground beside her.

"Forget it. It's too hot to ride," she said. "Let's walk down."

Kate grabbed the reins and led Mercury around to the barn.

"We can leave him here."

"I'm not sure we can get the doors open," Hallie said. "My dad says nobody's been in there for years."

"Don't worry about it," Kate said, winding the reins around a post. She picked up an old bucket and walked over to a pump Hallie had never even noticed before. After placing the bucket under the spigot, Kate began pumping the long, rusted metal arm up and down in quick movements, as if she thought water was really going to come out.

She's out of her mind, Hallie thought. But Kate kept pumping, and a few minutes later a few drops of rust-colored water trickled out of the pump. Kate increased the speed of her movements, and there was a gurgling sound, a cough from the belly of the pump, then a moment later water came pouring out.

When there was no more sign of rust, Kate filled the bucket and put it in front of Mercury.

Hallie was still staring at the pump when Kate walked back.

"Pump for me," she said.

"What?"

"Pump for me. I'm thirsty."

"We can go in the house and get a drink."

"Why bother?"

"I—I wouldn't drink this, if I were you."

"Why not?" Kate asked, amazed.

"It's—you know—"

"It's what?"

"Not purified."

Again Kate started laughing. "Pump."

Hallie took hold of the long arm of the pump and

moved it downward. A trickle of water came out. She moved it up again. It was much heavier than it looked.

"Faster," Kate commanded.

Hallie moved the handle up and down, but it was hard for her to get the right rhythm.

Finally, the water began coming out in bursts. Kate rinsed off her hands, then cupped them and drank great gulps of the clear water.

"Enough," she said, shaking her hands out. She ran the back of one hand across her mouth. Then she grabbed the handle from Hallie. "Try it."

Hallie hesitated.

"It's cleaner than the stuff you get from your sink in Los Angeles, or wherever it is you lived."

"I know that," Hallie said. "We drink bottled water."

"Well, where do you think that comes from?"

"I don't know."

"Wells," Kate pronounced. "Just like that one over there."

Hallie wasn't sure if she should believe Kate or not, but she was too embarrassed to walk away without at least tasting the well water.

She cupped her hands together as Kate had done, and she put them under the spigot. Cold, clear water bounced off them and splashed her legs. She jumped back, but she kept her hands outstretched until they were filled with water. Then she brought her hands to her mouth and drank, making great slurping sounds.

When she had finished drinking the water in her hands, she put them under the spigot again. Kate looked at her and smiled, then she started pumping again.

Instead of shaking out her hands when she was finished, Hallie patted her face and ran her fingers through her hair to cool off. The day had suddenly turned very warm.

"Ready?" Kate asked.

"Ready," Hallie answered as she followed Kate down the path she herself had taken to the stream.

"I've been down to the stream before," she said.

But when they got to the stream, Kate didn't stop, as Hallie had always done before.

They followed the stream for another mile into the woods where it suddenly broadened out into a pond deep enough to swim in.

Before they got to the water's edge, Kate pulled off her sweaty T-shirt and unzipped her shorts, and yanked them down. She was wearing a faded tank suit that clung to her body. She shook out her hair as they neared the water, and it streamed down her back like a mane.

"I didn't know—"

"You're right," Kate said, as she glanced over at Hallie. "It's too hot for clothes."

With one fluid movement, she pulled off her swimsuit and stepped out of it.

Hallie was too astonished to move. She looked away.

"I love to go skinny dipping," Kate said. But she didn't move either.

"It's too cold to swim," Hallie said.

"Up by your place, but not here," Kate said. "The sun warms it. This is the best time of the year for swimming here."

Hallie kept her eyes averted.

"Last one in's a jackass," Kate shouted, and she ran to the pond and jumped in.

As soon as Hallie heard the water splash, she looked

up. Kate was swimming across the pond, her head submerged in water.

Quickly, she undressed and folded her shorts and T-shirt. She hesitated for a moment, then stripped off her bra and panties, lay them on top of her clothes, and ran for the water, jumping in without hesitation, so it would cover her nakedness.

She swam smoothly, taking broad strokes, and soon she was almost up to Kate.

''You can see all the way to the bottom,'' Kate said, paddling along, waiting for Hallie to catch up.

Hallie dove under water, keeping her eyes open. Schools of tiny fish parted to let her through. She put her hand out to scoop them up, but they shifted direction and swam out of reach.

When she came up for air, she couldn't see Kate anywhere. She dove into the water again, and looked around, but couldn't find her. Maybe Kate was playing a joke on her. She remembered she had learned in school that Mercury was not only the god of transportation, he was a trickster, darting around, changing his shape to fool people. Suddenly, she was afraid that Kate had swum back to shore and taken her clothes.

Then, out of nowhere, Kate came from behind and swam underneath her, her body skimming Hallie's for a moment before she lunged forward, plunging in and out of the water like a dolphin heading toward the shore.

When Hallie came out of the water, Kate was lying on a rock, drying off. Her eyes were closed. Unable to control her own eyes, Hallie stared at Kate's body, and feeling her stare, Kate opened her eyes and smiled.

Hallie sat down on the rock beside Kate. She felt uncomfortable as Kate lay there, slowly studying her, just as Hallie had studied Kate. As nonchalantly as she could, Hallie crossed her arms in front of her breasts and held onto her shoulders.

"You get your period yet?" Kate asked.

"N-no," Hallie stammered.

"Didn't think so."

"Why?"

Kate sat up. Hallie stared into her eyes, so she could avoid looking at Kate's breasts, which were much more developed than hers. Who was this wild girl sitting so close to her that she could almost feel her breath on her face? She should have gone to Eugene with Jane and Molly, she thought. Even Jane's questions were safer than Kate's.

"Your buds are still too small," Kate said casually. "But don't worry. They'll blossom out. Look at mine. I graduated from a double A to an A over the summer, just before I got my period," she said.

Hallie understood that this was meant to be a simple statement of fact, and nothing more. But she was embarrassed by the intimacy.

"My sister's a C. She says that's the perfect size. I don't know. Who cares?" Kate asked rhetorically. Then she jumped up and ran toward the water again. "Time to cool off," she yelled, and she dove in.

Hallie sat watching her, transfixed. Kate bobbed in and out, blowing streams of water from her mouth, then shaking beads of liquid from her body as she strode back to the rock.

Kate stood there for a moment, then she leaned her head to the side, wiggled her finger in her ear, and stamped her foot.

"I better get back," Hallie said. "I forgot to leave a note for my dad."

"Shoot, he won't worry," Kate assured her. "Nothing could happen to you around here."

Chapter Seven

Hallie glanced at the clock. *Twelve-fifteen. The minutes were ticking away*. Over an hour had passed since she had sat down to fill in her columns. She hadn't gotten very far, but now, thinking about Kate, she felt wide awake. She leaned back in her desk chair and pictured Kate galloping past on Mercury. Kate was like the bushes that grew all around. She could sting you when you least expected it, but when she was riding, she looked light and airy, almost as though she had been picked up and carried along by the wind. Kate was a free spirit who sometimes understood the laws of nature better than the bonds of friendship.

Hallie had learned from experience that neither Kate nor the bushes were as fragile as they sometimes looked. When she tried to pull the dead plants up, she was surprised at their resistance. They left their marks on her arms and legs when she tried to uproot them.

She inspected her arms now to see if any of the scratches were still there. They weren't, but the memory of them was.

And so was the memory of going to school in Oregon. She picked up her pencil and wrote ''School'' in the plus column. She almost couldn't believe she had put it there. School had never been a very positive part of her life before.

Exactly how had it come about, she wondered now. It had seemed so natural back then. Her father had mentioned it very casually one day.

"Why not stay and go to the school here, Hallie? We'd love to have you."

She said her mother probably wouldn't be too thrilled with the idea, but when she called home and mentioned it to her mother, just as casually as her father had mentioned it to her, her mother didn't resist at all. She didn't actually push Hallie into staying, but she didn't seem too upset by the idea, either. Now, of course, Hallie realized why. Right after she had dropped Hallie off in Oregon and returned to California, her mother had met Frank. So when her father got on the phone and said, "Hallie's decided to stay here," Hallie didn't protest. But she did say that she had told her dad she'd try it for a year. She wanted to leave her options open. She wanted—she wasn't sure what she wanted.

But on some level, the idea of going to school in Oregon had probably entered her mind even before her father had brought it up. Looking back, she realized that the possibility had occurred to her that first day after she and Kate went swimming.

By the time they got back to her house, their hair and their bodies had completely dried off. There wasn't an ounce of water on them. It felt as if there weren't an ounce of water left in them, either. They were so parched from the sun.

They dragged themselves up the last few feet of the path, then walked around to the front door so they wouldn't bother her father, who was still working in his little room at the back of the house.

Hallie was disappointed when she saw Jane's car in the driveway. She wanted to keep Kate all to herself for a little longer. She thought about walking around back again and getting drinks from the pump, but before she could mention it to Kate, the front door swung open, and Jane's large frame filled the entrance way.

Hallie blushed as if she'd been caught doing something she shouldn't have been doing. She told herself there was no reason for her to be embarrassed. She hadn't done anything wrong. But, still, she had trouble looking Jane in the eye.

"Made some lemonade," Jane said. "And lunch."

"Thanks, Jane. I'm starving," Kate said easily, as if it was she who lived here, and not Hallie. "And about to die of thirst."

"When I saw your horse out back, I figured you two had gone for a walk," Jane said as the two girls followed her into the kitchen.

"We went all the way to the pond," Kate said after she had gulped down a glass of water. "You know where that is?"

"We used to take picnics there sometimes," Jane said, and she laughed. "In the good old days."

She poured two glasses of lemonade and set the sandwiches on the table in front of them. Then she poured herself a glass of lemonade and sat down across from Kate.

Hallie wondered if Kate would like the sandwich. Hallie didn't eat red meat. No one she knew in California did. Jane was strictly a sprouts and vegetables person, with some fish for protein occasionally. And Hallie's father went right along with her. He cut out articles from the newspaper about how beef was high in cholesterol and chicken was infested with salmonella and could make you sick, and articles about how a lot of beef was shipped in from other countries, and most of it wasn't even inspected. And when somebody or other tested the meat, they found it full of all kinds of terrible diseases, which, of course, turned Hallie's stomach. And besides what her father said, the thought of eating an actual animal that someone had slaughtered was too much for her. She wouldn't think of eating meat if her life depended on it, but other people didn't read those articles in the paper, so they might think serving a sandwich with just tomatoes, avocados, and sprouts for lunch was weird.

Kate didn't seem to notice. Or if she did, she was too hungry to say anything about it.

"Did you grow up around here?" she asked Jane.

"A few miles from here."

"I didn't know that."

"Well, I did, and I couldn't wait to get back."

"Yeah, I know what you mean," Kate said. "This is the best place to live. I mean, I might not live here all my life, but I'll probably always come back."

"Did your parents grow up around here?"

"Eugene. Both of them are from Eugene, but they lived in New York City for a while. I think they went to college there, or something. We go to New York every spring vacation. And every winter break we go to our house in Zermatt. Great skiing in Switzerland," Kate said, as she leaned forward to take another bite of her sandwich. "But I'm always glad to get back to Maplewood."

Hallie's mouth dropped open. Who was this person sitting at the table next to her? Was this the same country girl who had cupped her hands in order to drink well water?

"Your parents have a house in Switzerland?" Jane asked, as she leaned back in her chair.

"Yeah, and the apartment in New York. But I like it better here because—I don't know—maybe because you don't have to worry about anything, I guess. Like locking your doors, unlocking them, taking your radio out of the car so no one will steal it. Smells better here, too. At least, it smells better than it does in New York. The only thing wrong with Maplewood is there's no movie theater."

Hallie hadn't thought about that before. How do people live without going to movies, she wondered.

"Eugene's not so far," Jane said, and she laughed. "Except in winter, of course. Then it seems a hundred miles away."

Just when Hallie was congratulating herself for living in a city where she could walk to a movie theater if she wanted to, the conversation turned a corner. Hallie understood that somewhere along the way she had lost Kate's attention. Kate and Jane carried on as if they were girlfriends, and she was the outsider. And for the rest of the afternoon Hallie wondered what it would be like to live in Maplewood all year long. More precisely, she wondered what it would be like to go to school in Maplewood.

She couldn't help wondering about it. Not only had Kate and Jane grown up in the same area, but Kate went to the same school Jane had attended. This seemed to make them charter members of an exclusive club, and Hallie didn't even understand the terminology of that club. Jane mentioned that the school was consolidated. It took Hallie half the afternoon to figure out that consolidated meant that the school drew kids from the whole district, not just the immediate area. It seemed kids got to know everyone from miles around, and they got to go on hayrides, and to barn dances.

While Hallie knew vaguely what hayrides were, she had never heard of a barn dance, and couldn't imagine, at the time, how one danced in a barn—or for that matter why one would want to. But Jane and Kate talked on and on about how friendly everyone was, and about the way no one was ever left out because they all went around together in groups. Then Jane sighed, and said again that it was the best time of her life. And by this time, she and Kate were such good friends that when Kate said Jane looked much too young to be Hallie's mother, Jane laughed at the thought.

"I'm the big, bad stepmother," she said, only half-jokingly. "Wait till you meet Michelle, Hallie's real mother." She pronounced the name so that it sounded like "*Me*-Shell."

Hallie was so angry and hurt that she got up from the table and began clearing the dishes. She tried singing to herself to shut out the rest of the conversation, but, despite her attempt, she couldn't stop listening.

Luckily, Jane didn't say anything more about her mother, so Hallie could go back to feeling envious, rather than guilty. But she wasn't particularly proud of that, either.

Kate and Jane seemed to have endless things to say

about school, Hallie remembered, and she had even thought, at the time, that it sounded too good to be true. It sounded as if it wasn't easy enough to be boring, and it wasn't so hard that it occupied all your time.

Kate said she was on the basketball team.

"Me too," Jane said. "I was on the basketball team."

Big surprise, Hallie thought. I would hardly have expected her to say she took dance classes.

The next moment, Hallie inadvertently dropped a glass in the sink, and it splintered into a dozen pieces.

Chapter Eight

From what Kate had said that afternoon, Hallie knew that her family must have money. Lots of it. Later, after Kate had left, Jane told her that everyone knew the Evanses were the wealthiest family in town.

Hallie was surprised by Jane's acknowledgment. "Did you know they had an apartment in New York and a house in Switzerland?"

"Sure. This is a small town. Everybody knows everybody else's business."

"Then why didn't Kate know you weren't my real mother?"

"She probably did," Jane said nonchalantly.

"Then why—"

"Because that's the way it is. Even though you already know something, you pretend you don't. That way it doesn't seem like you're a gossip, and besides people have got to feel they have some privacy. Otherwise it could get pretty sticky."

Although she couldn't put her finger on exactly why, Hallie had been disturbed by the conversation, and she was even more upset when Jane carried on about Kate's family at dinner. In fact, she finally turned to her father and said, "Why do you care how much money Kate's family has, or where they go for their vacations?"

Both Jane and her father were quick to say it was just idle conversation. Of course, no one cared how much money anybody else had. That was one of the reasons they had moved to Maplewood, her father said. Here people were judged on their merits, not on their money.

"Why judge them at all?" Hallie had asked, as she got up to clear the table.

"Well, we don't really," Jane said. "That's just a figure of speech."

"Yes, we do," her father admitted. "We might not particularly like ourselves for doing it, but that's life, isn't it? People are judged by their accomplishments. I write a good book, people think I'm a good person. Your mother sells a poem or a painting, and people admire her. Someone else starts a soup kitchen for homeless people. Everyone thinks that person is wonderful."

"Can't a person be wonderful if she's just nice?" Hallie asked.

"No," her father answered. "Then she's just nice. Not wonderful."

"But whether or not you accomplish something, you're still the same person, aren't you?" Hallie asked.

"No, not really," her father said a little sadly. "Though we'd like to think so. If we're successful, if we have accomplished something worthwhile, we feel differently about ourselves. We act differently. People pick up on that, and they treat us differently. So, you see, it all comes down to the same thing in the end. We are judged on our merits. And we even judge ourselves that way. But in the end, I think it's better to be judged by what you've accomplished and not by the amount of money you've made accomplishing it.''

Hallie wasn't sure she liked her father's answer all that much, even though she tried not to take it personally. She had accomplishments. Her dance. Her dance teacher had told her mother she was gifted. Only that wasn't something her father counted as an accomplishment. To him, good grades were an accomplishment. Though good grades weren't something her mother cared about at all. Maybe because she hadn't been such a great student herself. From what her mother had said, Hallie suspected that she had some kind of learning disability. Only, of course, nobody knew anything about learning disabilities when her mother went to school.

In essence, Hallie decided as she scraped the food from her dish into the sink, what her father was saying was that you not only have to accomplish something, you have to accomplish something other people think is worthwhile, so they'll think you're more than just a nice person. Because, after all, who wants to be just nice? That was just about the worst thing you could say about anybody. If a friend asked you about somebody you thought was a loser, and you didn't want to be nasty, you'd say, ''Oh she's nice,'' or ''he's really a nice guy,'' which meant, of course, that she was probably not too bright, or he was really out of it.

When Hallie finished with her dish, she walked back to the table for her father's plate. When she came back for Jane's plate, she noticed that Jane's face had changed. That smile of contentment she usually wore had vanished, and Jane had a sort of strange look on her face. Not angry, or anything. Just empty. And when they heard Molly chirping, Jane quickly excused herself and didn't come downstairs again for the rest of the evening.

Chapter Nine

Kate taught her how to ride. At first she was afraid to mount the big gray mare that belonged to Kate's mother, but Kate assured her that Frida was the gentlest horse in their stable and had never thrown anyone.

And because Frida stood so patiently when Kate placed a saddle over her back, Hallie ignored her pounding heart, put her foot in the stirrup and let Kate help her boost herself up onto the saddle. Of course, after she was seated on the mare, she felt as if she were miles from the ground. And the reins felt so flimsy she couldn't understand how she could possibly control the horse with two narrow leather straps.

"Relax," Kate said, as she gracefully mounted her own horse. "We'll take it nice and slow. Maintain an easy walk."

Hallie tried to relax. She assumed just walking wouldn't be life threatening.

They took a trail that snaked alongside the Evans's property and into a heavily wooded area. Kate led the way, and Hallie followed her, gripping the horn of the saddle with all her might. It wasn't until they got to a clearing and could ride side by side that she realized she wasn't supposed to be clutching the horn.

"Let go of the saddle," Kate said. "Just hold lightly to the reins and use your thighs to grip the horse."

"But I'm afraid," Hallie admitted. At least the saddle horn felt secure. Besides, she had no idea how she was supposed to use her thighs to grip the horse.

"There's nothing to be afraid of. And remember, sit up straight," Kate said.

Hallie straightened her back and sat stiffly in the saddle, wondering how long this torture would continue. She felt as if they had been riding for hours, and she wished they could return to the stable, but Kate was oblivious of time and just kept advancing. The farther we ride, the longer it will take us to get back, Hallie kept thinking. But she was afraid to mention anything to Kate, who thought she was doing her a tremendous favor by teaching her how to ride.

Suddenly, they came into another clearing. Hallie's body ached both from the strain of sitting straight, as she had been instructed to do, and from the mordant fear that she would fall off the horse at any minute. Furthermore, her hands were sore from gripping the reins, and her bottom felt as if she had been beaten with a wooden board. But she smiled at Kate, and Kate smiled back at her and jumped off her horse.

Oh no, Hallie thought. I can't do that. She looked down at the ground, which seemed miles away. Getting off the horse seemed more dangerous than getting on.

When her feet finally touched the ground, she sighed with relief.

She didn't feel any sense of accomplishment. Only the dreadful realization that in order to get back to the stable, she would have to mount the horse again.

Kate undid the belt from around her waist and removed the cap of the canteen hanging from it. She handed the canteen to Hallie, who took a long drink of water and then returned it to Kate.

"I was born in a saddle," Kate said, and Hallie could almost believe she meant that literally. "Don't worry, you'll get the hang of it."

They walked over to a rock and sat down to relax. Hallie felt as if the insides of her thighs had been scraped raw. They felt wet, and her jeans were sticking to them. She imagined that by the time she got back, her thighs would probably be scarred for life. She'd never be able to put on shorts again.

"I never get tired of coming here," Kate said, staring into the distance.

Hallie followed Kate's eyes. Branches of trees on both sides of the trail overlapped, forming a filmy green ceiling. And the sun streamed in through open areas between the leaves sending thin shafts of light to the ground. Every time a breeze blew, the leaves shifted slightly, and the pattern of light changed.

It was so quiet here. Much quieter than it was in the city, which was never really quiet, even in the middle of the night. But this was the middle of the day, and the only sound was the song of distant birds.

"It's the light," Kate said, startling Hallie, who had lost track of time and place and was surprised to hear Kate's voice.

"When I come here at sunset, the light is totally different. I watch until the sun hits the leaves, then I quickly ride out to the pond and stand there until the sun goes down completely and the moon comes up," Kate said softly. "It's like magic. Maybe it is magic."

Hallie looked at Kate, afraid at first she might be

making fun of her, but she saw immediately that Kate was talking more to herself than she was to Hallie. That she, too, had been lost in her own thoughts.

"Why don't you rest for a few minutes. Mercury and I are going to take off. We'll be back in fifteen minutes," Kate said as she jumped into the saddle and tapped her heels against Mercury's sides. As if he were finally let free, the horse broke into a fast trot. Hallie watched as Kate leaned into him like a jockey, and Mercury began galloping.

Once again Hallie was struck by the strong, fluid connection between Kate and Mercury. She wondered if she would ever look as if she belonged on a horse.

When it was time for her to get back into the saddle, Hallie simply placed her foot in the stirrup and hoisted herself up without thinking. It just seemed like the natural thing to do.

The ride back was much shorter than the ride going. Hallie was almost disappointed when she spotted the stable in the distance.

Frida and Mercury must have spotted the barn at the same time. Mercury began trotting slowly, though Kate was holding him back, and Frida strained to follow.

"Let's just go home slowly, Frida," Hallie whispered. "Nice and easy."

Hallie shifted in the saddle. Her right foot accidentally hit the side of the horse, and as if that had given her permission to speed up, Frida also broke into a trot. As they approached the barn, Hallie kicked both sides of the horse, hoping to slow her down, but that simply spurred Frida on.

Hallie bobbed up and down on the hard saddle, crying, "Help! Help!" Over her shoulder, Kate yelled something in response, but she was too panicked to listen.

By the time they actually got back, she was clinging to Frida's neck, the horn of the saddle pushing into her stomach.

I will never get up on a horse again, she vowed, as Frida whinnied, slowed to a walk, and then stopped next to Mercury.

Laughing, Kate dismounted.

"Good girl," she said, giving Frida a slap on her right flank. "And good for you, too, Hallie. Your first lesson was a success. You even let Frida do a slow trot."

"I didn't *let* her," Hallie protested. "And it felt more like we were galloping."

Kate laughed again. "You'd know it if you were galloping. Believe me, you weren't riding as fast as you thought you were."

"Well, whatever it was, it was too fast for me."

"You can let go of Frida's neck now."

Hallie let go. She felt stiff, and when she tried to swing one leg over the saddle, she lost her balance and rolled off the horse.

She came down with a thud, but it wasn't a painful fall. Luckily, she had landed on a pile of hay next to the stable.

Kate knelt down next to her.

"You okay?"

"No."

"What hurts?"

"Everything."

"In general? Or from the fall?"

"In general."

"Good."

"Good? What's so good about it?"

"Hey, you just rolled off instead of stepping down. Actually, it looked kind of neat."

"Thanks." Hallie groaned as she sat up.

"Okay," Kate said. "Get back on."

"What?" Hallie said.

"Get back on. That's the rule."

"What rule?"

"If you fall off a horse, you have to get back on immediately."

"And whose rule is that?" Hallie asked, feeling shaky and disconcerted.

"It's a law of nature. If you fall off a horse, you have to get back on again right away, or you'll never have the nerve to try it again."

"I don't have the nerve to try it again now," Hallie said emphatically. She started walking toward Kate's house. Her knees were shaking, and she felt as if the saddle were still between her legs. All she could think about was calling her father to come pick her up. She had had enough of horses for one day. She'd probably had enough of horses forever.

Kate led Frida up alongside her, and Frida nuzzled her hand, as if she were trying to apologize. Kate put something into Hallie's hand. Hallie stopped walking and looked down. It was a lump of sugar.

"Give it to her," Kate said. "She's sorry you fell; aren't you, girl?"

Hallie looked at Kate.

"Really."

Hallie opened her hand and watched as the horse's mouth moved toward it. Frida gratefully accepted the lump of sugar, then nodded her head up and down and licked Hallie's hand. "Come on," Kate said, trying to encourage her. "I'll lead Frida. All you have to do is sit there."

Hallie hesitated. Then reluctantly, she put her foot into the stirrup and swung her leg over the saddle one more time. Frida stood perfectly still.

"Remember, if you want a horse to slow down, pull on the reins and yell."

"I did yell," Hallie protested. "I yelled 'help.' "

"Try 'whoa' next time," Kate said.

"Should have told me that before," Hallie mumbled as Kate picked up the reins and led Frida slowly around the stable.

"I tried to," Kate said.

And this time when Hallie dismounted, both feet hit the ground, which didn't seem as far away as it had the first time she dismounted.

Chapter Ten

When Hallie's father had dropped her off in front of Kate's, Kate had been waiting for her. They'd walked around back to the stables right away, so she had never actually been inside the house. As they trudged up to the back door, she was vaguely curious about just how many rooms the huge, old Victorian house contained. But because she was having trouble putting one foot in front of the other, she was more curious about whether or not she would actually make it inside.

"Maybe you'll be lucky and get to meet my sister," Kate said as she opened the back door.

"Your sister?" Hallie asked, once again conscious of the searing pain in her thigh muscles.

"C cup. Remember?"

"Yeah," Hallie said. How could she forget?

"We're back," Kate yelled. "Anybody home?"

No one answered, but Hallie could hear rock music coming from someplace in the house.

"She's probably upstairs admiring herself," Kate said.

Hallie followed Kate through the kitchen, which she noticed was very modern despite the fact that it was built to look old-fashioned.

They climbed the stairs—Kate with ease, Hallie with great difficulty. Kate banged on the only door in the long hallway that was closed.

A few seconds later the music got softer, and someone yelled, "Enter."

"This is my friend, Hallie," Kate said. "And this is my sister."

Kate's sister said, "Hi," and Hallie said, "Hello."

Then Kate's sister laughed. "I also have a name. I'm Deirdre."

Hallie was embarrassed. She knew she was staring at Deirdre, but she couldn't help it. If she looked like her, she'd be up in her room admiring herself, too.

"You guys ride out to the meadow?" Deirdre asked.

"Yeah," Kate said.

"Figured."

"Why's that?"

Deirdre smiled and nodded at the floor.

Hallie almost fainted. They had tracked mud onto the shiny, ash-colored wooden floor.

"No big deal. I'll go get some paper towels," Kate said, and she walked back downstairs.

Hallie didn't know if she was supposed to follow her, or not. She shifted from one leg to the other. They'd made a real mess.

"Take your shoes off and come in, if you want to," Deirdre said.

Gratefully, Hallie leaned against the wall so she could kick off her shoes. She wanted to cry out because of the pain in her legs when she lifted each of them up, but she knew that would be very uncool. Still, she couldn't help wincing.

"You like hard rock?" Deirdre asked.

Hallie didn't really. She liked soft rock. She also liked classical music because that's what she listened to when she practiced ballet.

"Yeah, I love it," she said.

Deirdre shoved aside a pile of clothes on her bed. "Sit down if you want to."

"I'm probably sort of smelly from riding," Hallie said reluctantly. There was nothing she would have liked more than to sit down on Deirdre's bed and pretend they were old friends.

"No big deal," Deirdre assured her. Hallie sat down next to Deirdre, and she realized Deirdre's own jeans smelled like she'd been riding in them—more than once. She was so natural. That was so cool.

As Deirdre plowed her way through a stack of CD's, Hallie surreptitiously watched her.

She didn't look anything like Kate. Her hair was dark. So dark it looked almost black, but not the way hair looks when it's dyed. Then it's purplish. And there was lots of it. It was long and heavy and very curly. Her skin was dark, too, so when she looked at you with her light green eyes, it almost came as a shock. Hallie tried to sneak a look at her famous C cup, but Deirdre was wearing a big work shirt over her T-shirt.

Hallie was almost disappointed when Kate returned a few minutes later, her hands stuffed with wet paper towels.

"I guess I got most of it. Let's go down and make ourselves a snack."

"See you around," Deirdre said as Hallie got up from the bed.

Hallie tripped over one of Deirdre's shoes as she headed for the door.

"Sorry," she said.

"Just pick it up and throw it over there with the other one," Deirdre said.

Hallie followed her glance to a pile of shoes in the corner of the room.

"Throw it?"

"Or just leave it there. It doesn't matter."

Which should she do, Hallie wondered. Before she could decide, Kate picked up the stray shoe and tossed it across the room. It landed on a pile of dirty underwear.

"Your sister's gorgeous," Hallie whispered as they walked down the stairs.

"Yeah, she's not bad," Kate said, but Hallie knew that Kate was pleased that she'd noticed. How could anyone help but notice?

When they got to the bottom of the steps, Hallie saw that there were streaks of mud, only half washed away. "Maybe we better clean this up," she said. "I'll help you."

"Nah, forget it," Kate assured her.

"Will your maid do it?"

Kate burst into laughter. "Nobody around here has a maid," she said. "Believe me, no one else will even notice."

Hallie looked into the living room. Piles of books and newspapers were stacked all over. Some of them weren't even stacked. They lay on tables and chairs, half covering a sweater or jacket or a crumpled pair of socks.

And the kitchen wasn't much different. Though it was generally neater, Hallie saw dirty dishes in the sink and two bags of garbage next to the refrigerator.

There was something very liberating about the mess. As if Kate's family didn't really care if they were rich. As if they barely even noticed.

Chapter Eleven

It was one-thirty. Hallie looked down at her paper. She focused on "School" in the plus column. She'd let her mind drift again, and once more she realized how natural it had been to make the decision to stay in Oregon for school last year. It had just sort of happened. And before she knew it, the first day of school had rolled around, and she was walking to the school-bus stop.

On her way, she kept reassuring herself that she had made the right decision. But by the time she got on the bus, she felt awkward and apprehensive. Her stomach muscles tightened. She didn't know any of the kids in Maplewood, except Kate. Suddenly, she wished she hadn't let her father talk her into staying. She wished she had taken more time to make her decision. Maybe she had made a mistake. Maybe she should get off at the next stop, walk home, and tell her father she wanted to fly back to California immediately.

She started to rise out of her seat as soon as the bus began slowing down. Then a dash of red caught her eye, and she looked out the window and saw Kate jumping up and down, waving to her. She smiled, returned the wave, and happily sank back down into her seat, as if she had simply stood up to make sure her friend was at the bus stop.

When she boarded, Kate waved to the kids already on the bus, shouting, "Hi, guys" to some of them. They all cheerfully shouted various greetings back to her. Except for a tall, blond-haired boy Hallie had noticed, who was slouched in his seat near the front of the bus. Kate seemed to ignore him completely.

Hallie held her breath, praying that Kate would sit down next to her. She slid over, as close to the window as possible, silently inviting her to occupy the empty space beside her.

Kate walked toward her, then stopped next to another girl. Hallie's heart started beating faster and faster. She knew she had no right to expect Kate to sit with her. Kate had other friends. She obviously had lots of other friends. Hallie felt miserable.

The bus started moving again. "Everybody grab a seat now," the driver commanded. And in a flash, as if she had been heading toward Hallie all along, Kate pivoted, walked across the aisle and sat down next to her.

She pointed to various kids, imperiously reeling off their names, as if, until that very moment, they had been nameless, and it was up to Kate to designate what each of them would be called. Hallie couldn't begin to keep them straight. She remembered some of the names, but she couldn't remember to which faces they belonged.

She waited for Kate to complete the naming process. But when Kate went on to another subject, Hallie realized she wasn't going to mention the blond boy sitting near the front of the bus.

"What's that girl's name, the one sitting across from us?" Hallie whispered.

"Melanie," Kate said. "She's a ninth grader," she added, as if to dismiss her as a possible friend.

"And the blond kid sitting near the front of the bus?" Hallie asked, her voice barely audible.

"Joanne? You mean the girl three seats down?"

"The guy in front of her."

"Oh, that's Peter Gates," Kate said nonchalantly.

"Do you know him?"

"Everybody knows everybody around here." Kate shrugged her shoulders as if to ward off further questions. Then she turned to the girl in the seat in back of theirs and said, "This is Hallie." She poked Hallie, and Hallie turned around and smiled at the girl. The girl smiled back. "You're from California, huh?"

It was clear the girl already knew Hallie's complete history. It made Hallie feel a bit strange. She wondered what Kate had said about her, and what, in fact, there was to say.

The bus stopped seven or eight more times before reaching the school, and as kids hopped on, they added to the general pandemonium.

As the bus pulled into the school driveway, Hallie was swept along by the enthusiasm of all the kids around her, and she was only vaguely conscious of the fact that every student on the bus was white.

Even though it was way past her usual bedtime Hallie now felt totally awake. She remembered how happy she had been that first day of school. It was perfect.

She had never been the center of attention anywhere in her life before. Not even in her dance classes. But on the first day at school everyone seemed to notice her. Even the ninth graders. Many kids waved or said hello to her. Lots of them came up to talk to her, in her classes and at lunch. By the end of the day, everyone seemed to know who she was.

Somehow it didn't seem to matter all that much if her privacy had been invaded. She felt as if she had been drawn into a circle of warmth, and the price of one's privacy was little enough to pay. Smiles of unconditional acceptance spread across people's faces when she met them, teachers and kids. Girls, buzzing around, hovered over her as if Kate had cut a path for her, and all Hallie had to do was walk down it and gather the honey.

To her added delight, Hallie found the work easy. She'd already covered most of it last year. So as she boarded the bus to return home that first day, she felt almost light enough to float up the steps and into a seat. She knew she could conquer her homework with ease. This was also a first for her.

When they reached Kate's stop, Hallie asked her if she wanted to ride on to her house.

"Sure," Kate said. "Deirdre can pick me up later."

And, just as if she'd been going to school in Maplewood forever, Hallie hopped down the steps of the bus with her best friend when it pulled up at her stop. They trudged up to her house, their book bags strapped to their backs, chattering nonstop about every detail of the day. They had English, social studies and gym classes together.

"You've got to try out for the basketball team," Kate said. "That's the best girls' team. I'm on it."

"But I've never played basketball. I mean I've fooled around with my dad at the schoolyard, but I've never really played. I'm not very athletic, I guess," Hallie said, her voice trailing off.

"You never rode a horse before either," Kate assured her.

"Yeah, but—"

"You're tall. We need you. You're trying out. Period."

"But—"

"Period."

"When do you practice?"

"Between three and four-thirty every day. There's a late bus for kids involved in after-school activities, so don't worry, you'll be able to get home."

"That's not what I was thinking about," Hallie said. "It's just that—well—at home—I mean when I lived in Venice, I took dance classes four days a week after school and on Saturdays. I guess I should start looking for a place to study here. I'm beginning to get out of practice."

"You *study* dance?" Kate asked.

"Ballet."

"Ballet," Kate repeated, as if it were a foreign word.

"So I won't have time for basketball."

"Uh-huh," Kate said, as if she didn't really believe Hallie. It made her feel uncomfortable.

They went into the kitchen and poured themselves glasses of milk. Jane had baked some oatmeal cookies that they stuffed into their mouths before sitting down at the table.

"Good," Kate said. "My mom used to bake, but she gave it up. I forget why. I don't know. Maybe she got too fat, or something."

"You found the cookies," Jane said, walking into the kitchen carrying Molly.

"Weren't we supposed to eat them?" Hallie asked, as she guiltily wiped some crumbs from her mouth.

"Of course you were supposed to eat them," Jane said. "This is your house, too, Hallie. You're not just a guest here."

Hallie smiled weakly. She still felt like a guest.

"Can I hold her?" Kate begged.

Jane turned the baby over to Kate, and Kate bounced her around as she and Hallie rehashed the day with Jane.

"Miss Hargrave was my eighth grade teacher," Jane yelled at one point. "I can't believe it."

"And you said you were on the basketball team, too," Kate said to her.

"I played center," Jane said proudly. "We went to the state finals three years in a row."

"It would be great if Hallie could play," Kate said.

"Why couldn't she?"

"I thought I should—"

"Ballet," Kate answered for her.

That annoyed Hallie, though she couldn't put her finger on exactly why. It just seemed as if every time Kate came over, she and Jane carried on their own private conversation, forgetting Hallie was even in the room.

"Gee, honey," Jane said sweetly, "I forgot all about your dancing."

"Yeah, I guess I better start working on it again."

"Can't you do it in the evenings. After dinner?"

"Most of the classes are after school. At least they were at home."

"Classes," Jane mumbled, as if she were processing what Hallie was saying for the first time.

She walked over to the phone book and opened it up to the yellow pages. Before Hallie could warn her that wasn't the way you went about finding a dance teacher, Jane announced that there were no ballet classes in Maplewood. At least none were listed in the phone book. The closest ballet schools were in Eugene.

"I don't know, hon, that's a long way to drive more than once a week. But maybe if your dad and I took turns—"

"I could take a bus," Hallie volunteered.

Jane and Kate exchanged glances. "It would take you almost two hours just to get there by bus."

It was almost as if they were in collusion. As if everyone was in collusion against her continuing to dance. The knot in Hallie's stomach was so tight she thought she might explode at any minute. But she just smiled at Jane and Kate, and said, "Well—maybe we can work something out."

She couldn't sleep that night either, Hallie remembered. The day had somehow turned on her. All during dinner she'd waited for Jane to bring up her dance classes, but Jane had a million other things to discuss with her father, and Hallie was almost afraid to bring it up herself. If she put off talking to him about it, she could put off hearing his opinion on the matter.

When he came in to say good-night to her she was going to say something. She started to.

"Dad—"

"Ummm," he said, in that distracted way he had sometimes.

"I was wondering—"

"Ummm-hummm?"

"Nothing."

"What, honey?"

Molly started to cry.

"I have to get her," her father said. "Jane's exhausted."

"Night, Dad," Hallie said. She reached up for her light and turned it off before he had a chance to see the tear that for some strange reason, was rolling down her cheek.

"Was it something important, Hallie?"

"No," she said. She hoped he hadn't heard her voice quivering.

"Good night. Don't let the bed bugs bite."

She heard him blow her a kiss from the door, but her eyes were closed tightly, so she didn't see him pull it shut.

Chapter Twelve

Hallie leaned forward, her whole body alert, eyes straight ahead, ready to receive the ball. Juneann passed it to Kate, and Kate lobbed it over to her. She took it and dribbled across the floor, easily weaving in and out of the players on the opposing side. Then, with all eyes on her, she stood poised in front of the basket for a split second. She lifted her arms, aimed carefully, and took a shot. The spectators on the visitors' side of the auditorium screamed their approval as the ball hit the backboard, then sped through the hoop.

A slow smile crept across Hallie's face as she watched the scoreboard change. This was the first basket she'd made in public. Two of her teammates quickly patted her on the back as they began chasing after the star of the opposing team, who now had the ball.

Hallie wished they could have taken just one more moment to let her bask in her accomplishment. There was something very heady about listening to people cheering for her—just for her. But there was no time for more than a couple of "nice jobs."

Kate jumped higher than anyone else and grabbed the

ball, and then dribbled it down the court as Clarkdale, the opposing team, clamored after her. Just as two of them outpaced her and placed themselves in front of her, their arms waving up, down, and around, she whirled and threw the ball to Hallie, who was just as surprised by the tricky move as the opposite team. By instinct more than by intellect, she performed a flying leap, grabbed the ball, and gracefully landed on two feet before delivering it to Samantha with one fluid motion.

As Samantha dribbled down the court with it, spectators rose to their feet, screaming, "Go! Go!" And just as she reached the basket and dunked the ball, the buzzer went off, signifying the end of the first half.

Both teams retired to the sidelines, still wired with energy. The score was 27 to 17, with Clarkdale in the lead.

"Great game. Great game," Coach Reily said.

"What do you mean, 'great game'? We're losing," Juneann reminded her.

"You were just warming up. You'll trounce them next period."

"Can you believe that move Kate made?"

"The ball was out of her hand before Clarkdale knew she had thrown it."

"They were all over her, but she moved so fast, it was like a sleight-of-hand trick. Now you see the ball. Now you don't. And all of a sudden, before anyone realized Kate wasn't even holding the ball anymore, Hallie was receiving it."

"Now that was something to see," Coach Reily said.

"You looked like a ballet dancer, leaping up in the air for that ball."

Suddenly, the attention shifted from Kate to her, and Hallie felt a ripple of excitement surge through her stomach. She smiled a little nervously.

"Thanks," she said quietly. But her stomach churned with excitement.

At that moment, three-fourths of the school descended on the court and started yammering away, rehashing the last half and encouraging the team on to victory.

Hallie joined the commotion, but she couldn't help noticing Peter Gates, the blond boy she'd seen on the bus the first day of school, and every day since. He stood several feet away from them, but even if he had been in the middle of the crowd, he would have stood out. Not because he had to, but because he obviously wanted to. Hallie knew that, but she didn't know how she knew it. He simply looked sure of himself, as if he had more important things to think about than basketball. Still, he was here. Something had brought him to the game.

"Hey, Gates," another boy, George Davis, shouted, "maybe we can recruit Evans and Barns for the boys' team."

"Don't hold your breath, Davis," Kate shouted, but she didn't look at Peter, and Peter didn't respond to George.

But Hallie felt herself blushing with pride at being singled out by George. He had not only acknowledged that she played a good game, he knew her name. And he was a ninth grader!

Some of the other kids wandered over to Peter. Hallie

watched him as he talked to them, measuring out his words. She couldn't hear the conversation, but she could see that he wasn't saying much despite the fact that everyone was focused on him.

"You're coming, aren't you, Barns?" George asked her, pulling her back to the conversation that had been going on around her.

She knew her face looked blank, but she had no idea what he was talking about.

"Sure, she's going," Kate answered for her. "Everyone's going, aren't they?"

"I'm going. Rogers is going. Milford is going. Michaels is going," George said. He smiled at Kate, a funny little smile, as if he were half teasing her, but Hallie didn't understand what he was teasing her about, and where it was they were all going, including her, it seemed.

She did know that Kate knew she was being teased, however, because she looked at George with exaggerated disgust to let him know she knew, but she wasn't really mad at him.

"And Smith is going," George went on. "And Reynolds."

"Okay," Kate said, getting a little irritated now. "We get the point."

But Hallie didn't get the point at all.

"And Gates," George said, ignoring Kate. "That is—Gates will probably be there, depending—"

"I don't care if Gates will be there, or not," Kate said, her face turning as red as her hair.

"Okay, team, let's cut the chatter now," Coach Reily yelled. She motioned them toward her, and the other kids drifted off the court and back to their seats. "A few instructions before the next quarter."

They pinned down some strategic points, patted each other on their backs, and broke just as the whistle blew.

"Where is it we're all going?" Hallie asked, as she and Kate angled their way onto the floor toward the referee.

"Eyes up!" Coach Reily yelled before Kate had a chance to answer.

The game got under way again, and it wasn't until the fourth period, when they were leading 43 to 38, and Coach Reily replaced Hallie and Kate with second stringers, that she remembered the earlier conversation.

"Where are we going, and when?" she asked again.

"You were standing there. You heard the conversation as well as I did," Kate said matter-of-factly, as her eyes followed Juneann down the court toward the basket.

"But—"

Juneann paused, aimed momentarily, and shot. The ball rimmed the basket, but didn't fall into it.

"Damn," Kate said. "She never takes enough time to set it up. She just has to learn there are certain things that just need time. You can't push them," she mumbled.

Hallie was about to comment when she realized that Kate was talking more to herself than to Hallie.

They won the game hands down. And afterward they piled into the Evans's van and headed back to Maplewood.

As Hallie sat down in the backseat, she felt something under her leg. She reached for it and retrieved a social studies text book. She opened it up and absent-mindedly thumbed through it.

Someone had drawn a heart in the margin of one of the pages. It was too dark to see it clearly until they stopped at a light. Then Hallie almost cried out in surprise. In the middle of the heart were the initials K.E. and P.G.

K.E. and P.G. They didn't even like each other. They went out of their way to avoid talking to each other. Hallie was totally shocked. Someone must have played a joke on Kate.

She closed the book quickly and studied the back of Kate's head for some clue.

"So wait till you tell your dad and Jane, Hallie," Kate said, turning around.

Hallie quietly dropped the book to the floor of the car.

"Keeping up the family tradition."

"Yeah," Hallie said. "Keeping up the family tradition." She wasn't about to point out that Jane wasn't really part of her family. Then she realized that if Jane was part of her dad's family, and she was part of her dad's family, Kate was right in a way. In a sort of complicated way, which she wasn't sure she was quite ready to accept, they were part of the same family.

When Hallie got home, she got another surprise. Jane and her dad had papered the downstairs with signs saying things like CONGRATULATIONS, and HALLIE BARNS, BASKETBALL STAR.

"How did you know?" she asked, bewildered.

"We heard the results of the game on the ten o'clock news," her father said.

"On the news? Our game was on the news?"

"Sure. It's the most important local news of the day," Jane said.

"Maybe the most important national news, too," her father said. "Aside from the dissolution of the Soviet Union."

"Wow," Hallie said. "We were on the news."

"I'm so sorry we couldn't make it," her father said. "What a time to get the flu."

"You shouldn't have worn yourself out making all those signs," Hallie said. Then she smiled. "But I'm glad you did."

"There was even a shot of you and Kate," Jane said.

"That was some leap," her father added.

"You saw it? I can't believe you really saw it."

Hallie remembered how she had leapt up into the air and cheered. She had felt so good. It made her feel good all over again, just thinking about it now. She raised her hands in a victory salute and gave a silent cheer. Then she wrote "basketball" in the plus column.

"Yes," she said to herself. "Yes. Yes. Yes." But somewhere inside of her, something was nagging at her, saying, "Not quite, my friend. Not quite." And slowly the rest of the evening came back to her.

"Well, I guess all your dancing finally paid off," her father said. "No one but a dancer could have made that leap."

"It was so fun," Hallie said. But her words suddenly seemed hollow.

"I'm going to call Mom and tell her," she said, trying to recapture the excitement.

And it worked for a few minutes. She could hear her voice get higher and higher as she went through each period of the game, telling her mother how everyone had stood up and cheered for her and Kate. And when she told her mother how much fun it was, she was telling the truth.

"That's great," her mother said. "I'm so proud of you."

"Me too," Hallie admitted.

"But are you dancing, Hallie?"

"Not much," she answered guiltily.

"You have to keep in shape," her mother reminded her.

"I know," Hallie said. And she hung up the phone and sighed, feeling her stomach muscles tighten.

As she thought about the phone call, Hallie could feel her stomach muscles tightening now, too.

Whenever her mother reminded her to practice, she would run through her ballet steps and try all the positions for the next few days, but she had no bar in Maplewood on which to practice, and, in the end, they all decided that Eugene was just too far away, though Jane or her father had driven her there once a week for three weeks. But then the baby was sick, and her father was busy, and she knew that nobody really wanted to drive her.

Hallie started to erase basketball from the plus column, but she couldn't. It *was* a positive experience. She had loved playing, loved being part of the team. And it hadn't really kept her from dancing. Maybe, in a way, she had kept herself from it.

Chapter Thirteen

Hallie shivered under her light, cotton pajamas. *It was after two*, and the room had grown damp and cold. It had also been chilly in the big barn the night of the dance, Hallie remembered. But no one complained. The excitement in the air seemed to warm everyone up. Kids were all talking at once, but Hallie wasn't sure if anyone was really listening. Talking itself seemed enough to give the group a feeling of communion. It didn't really matter what the words were.

Hallie had the same feeling she had had when her mother took her to a Bruce Springsteen concert. The whole audience had been collectively transported to the same place by his music. And it was almost as if everyone was connected by an invisible golden string. After the concert, people smiled and talked to each other, verifying the experience, though there was an unspoken recognition that the words didn't mean anything in particular. It was the underlying feeling that mattered. People were simply making connections. Hallie realized that was exactly what she and the other kids were doing as they greeted each other in the barn.

The big space, empty of everything except bales of

hay pushed in corners and pitchforks and old wagon wheels leaning against the walls, had been swept clean for the dance. Until now Hallie hadn't realized that a barn dance was actually held in a real barn.

Everyone in the eighth and ninth grades seemed to be here, and, as usual, Kate was at the center of a group of kids. Hallie smiled, feeling good about being close to someone who was so popular.

She looked around the room, wondering if anyone would ask her to dance.

"They're here," Juneann's mother announced as she walked into the barn with two men. One carried a violin case. The second, a much older man, just smiled and looked around as the younger man took out his instrument.

How were they supposed to dance to a violin, Hallie wondered.

"Form your squares," the older man said. "For those of you who don't know me, I'm Dave, your caller. And this here is Rob on the fiddle."

What in the world was the man talking about Hallie wondered, as the kids around her broke up into groups.

"Uh-uh," Dave said, and he laughed. "None of this girl, girl stuff. Boy, girl, boy, girl. None of them boys is going to bite you ladies, and none of these fine young ladies is going to trap you young gentlemen. So get yourselves a partner of the opposite sex and form your squares so we can get started."

While Hallie was still trying to figure out what was going on, George Davis grabbed her arm and pulled her over to a group standing nearby. Once she and George joined them, they completed a square with a boy and girl standing together forming each of the sides of the square. There were a few feet of empty space in the middle.

Everyone was scurrying around to form other squares, except for Kate and Peter. Kate was talking to Juneann's mother and Peter was just hanging around watching everyone else.

"Okay, you two," Dave shouted. "We're two people short over here. Grab that young man over there, Red, and we can get started."

Without looking at Peter, Kate ambled over to the square with the missing couple and stood in place. The other kids in the square called to Peter, but he seemed reluctant to join them.

Finally, Monty, another ninth-grade boy, broke out of the group, walked over to Peter and grabbed his jacket. Peter laughed good-naturedly, as if he'd been caught and there was nothing he could do about it. He let Monty pull him into the square next to Kate. But he refused to look at her, and she refused to look at him.

Just her luck, Hallie thought. Kate obviously couldn't stand Peter, but Hallie would have given anything at that moment to be standing in Kate's place.

"Okay," Dave shouted, as Rob stood poised, ready to play. "Anyone here who's never done any square dancing? Raise your hand if you're city folk and ain't never had the pleasure."

Hallie looked down at the floor, but she knew that no one had raised a hand. She didn't raise hers either. She could feel people staring at her. Her partner even nudged her, but she refused to raise her hand and make a fool out of herself.

"We'll begin with an easy one, just to refresh your

memory and get you all started," Dave said. "The Virginia Reel."

Rob began playing and stamping his foot immediately. Hallie had never heard music like this before. She wasn't sure how people danced to it. To her surprise, no one seemed to move. They just stood there, looking straight ahead.

I'm a dancer, she thought, I can follow George. I'll just wait to see what he does, and I'll do the same thing. George stood perfectly still. So Hallie stood perfectly still, though she felt like tapping her foot to the music.

"Honor your partner," Dave shouted.

Hallie almost burst out laughing at such a silly thought. It sounded like something from the Bible.

But before she had a chance to wonder exactly what that meant, George turned to her and bowed. Her eyes almost popped out of her head. Then she realized every other boy in the square was bowing to his partner, and the girls were curtsying, holding out pretend dresses, since they were all wearing jeans. She curtsied, too.

"Honor your corners all," Dave shouted.

George turned away from her and bowed to Sue, who was part of the couple standing next to them. Ron tapped her on the shoulder and bowed to her. She curtsied to him.

"Now swing that partner to and fro and get in place for a do-si-do."

George linked his arm through hers, and they swung around. "Keep your arm extended half way and put your hand at your waist," George whispered.

Hallie laughed. This was fun. She was square dancing.

When they had swung around for a few minutes, they stood in their places again. Everyone folded their arms across their chests. Hallie followed. Then each girl skipped past her partner, circled around him, and came back into place. Then each boy did the same thing as Dave called "Do-si-do your partner."

By the time they started the next dance, Hallie could follow most of the directions and swung in and out, around the square just like the other kids. She could honor her partner, honor her corner, do-si-do, run to the middle and back and collapse with laughter along with everyone else.

When Dave announced they were ready to take a little break, she was sorry. It was such fun. Once she got used to the music and Dave's calling out the instructions, she relaxed and really got into it. It was almost like a version of rap. Talking with the music instead of singing.

Laughing, clapping, heated from dancing, hungry and thirsty, they all gathered around an oblong plank, that was supported by wooden horses on either end and covered with a checkered paper cloth. Juneann's parents had set up a makeshift table laden with huge bowls of ice cream and a dozen different toppings. Hot chocolate, marshmallows, M&M's, Heath-bar chips, butterscotch. It was a feast, an ice cream festival. They all dug in, making complete pigs of themselves.

The decibel level was lowered for a few minutes while they wolfed down their sundaes; then it rose again as the first ones to finish eating started joking around.

When Dave and Rob finished eating, they walked back to the area they had staked out as theirs, and Dave called out, "Pick your partners and form your squares.

Choose a different partner from the one you had before, ladies and gentlemen, and get yourselves ready to dance.''

There was general commotion while everyone scampered around looking for a new partner. Hallie scanned the room, searching for Peter. She couldn't find him— or Kate. She scanned the room again, letting her eyes rest on the few kids still standing near the table eating, then on the groups of squares already formed, but neither of them were in the room.

Donny Scott, who had been Sue's partner, walked over to her and said, ''We need another girl.''

It wasn't much of an invitation and not the invitation she was looking for at all, but Hallie didn't know how to turn Donny down graciously, so she followed him to a square with one empty side and got into place.

Just as Rob placed his violin—which Dave called a fiddle—under his chin, she saw Kate slip into the barn from outside. Her face was all red, as if she'd been running. A cold draft swept through the barn, and Hallie noticed that Kate had left the door slightly ajar, but she didn't move from her place to close it. Instead, she followed Kate with her eyes as she took her place in another group. For a moment, Hallie wondered how Kate was going to dance without a partner.

Then she felt another blast of cold air before the door was finally shut tightly. Peter walked into the barn and took his place beside Kate. The music started, and Dave called out, ''Honor your partner.''

As Hallie curtsied to Donny, she looked over at Kate, who was smiling at Peter. It was a strange kind of smile, Hallie thought, for someone who didn't really like someone else. Then the smile was gone, and Kate lifted her head in the air and whinnied. Or at least that's what it looked like.

And when they went once around the hall together, Hallie noticed that Peter kept his arm around Kate's shoulder just a moment too long.

"God, I can't believe you got stuck with Peter for the whole evening," Hallie said to Kate as they were getting into her father's car.

"Who says I was stuck with him?" Kate snapped.

"But I thought you didn't like him."

"Guess you thought wrong," Kate said, and she laughed as she got into the backseat and pulled the door closed after her.

Hallie was totally confused. She started to remind Kate that she had always acted like she didn't like Peter, then she changed her mind. Maybe it was one of those things she'd understand once she got her period.

Chapter Fourteen

Hallie's eyes wandered back up the column to "School." She hadn't missed one day last year. Everything about school had been fun. Even the work. Maybe because she'd already done most of it in L.A. in seventh grade. And Mrs. Smith was so nice. She never called on kids unless they raised their hands, so no one had to panic about being embarrassed in front of the whole class.

Hallie remembered how proud she was when she got her first report card last fall. All A's. She'd never, ever gotten all A's before. Maybe because she had missed quite a bit of school in L.A. Usually on days when they had tests. Especially vocabulary tests which she sometimes forgot to make up. She got B's and C's mostly. It made her feel bad. Not that her mother put pressure on her to do better. She didn't. "Your grades are fine, Hallie," she'd say. "You're a lot smarter than I was when I was your age."

But when everyone compared grades, she felt kind of stupid. And some days she had a hard time facing Ms. Crandle. "If you people can't learn these vocabulary words," Ms. Crandle used to say, "how do you expect to do well on the S.A.T. exam?"

That used to throw everybody at her old school into a panic. And it made Hallie think of children's stories where people warn kids about big, bad wolves. But no matter how often she was warned, or how hard she studied, Hallie couldn't seem to remember what words like "synergism" or "hubris" meant.

But eighth grade in Oregon was different. They had words like "expectation" and "suspect" on their vocabulary tests. She had no trouble remembering what those words meant. And no one in her class had even heard of the Scholastic Aptitude Test. Kate's sister knew what it was, but she said she didn't care about it all that much. She was going to the University of Oregon. And as long as she kept her grades up, she'd get in.

Hallie felt tremendous relief.

Even if she went to school in Los Angeles in the fall, she could still go to the University of Oregon if she wanted to.

When she brought her report card home from school, she tried not to show Jane how excited she was. It was so uncool to be excited about something like grades. And besides, she really wanted to tell her father about it first. But Jane, being Jane, sensed that something was up.

"Whatcha got there?" she asked.

"Just my report card," Hallie said, blushing.

"Can I take a look at it?"

"If you want to," Hallie said. She was too embarrassed to refuse, and she didn't want to hurt Jane's feelings.

"Wow!" Jane said after she looked at the report card.

"You've got a very smart sister, Molly," she said, turning to the baby. "Think you'll do this well when you go to school?"

Molly let out a shriek, and Jane and Hallie burst out laughing.

"Guess she doesn't like to be compared to her older sister, even now," Jane said.

It was because of the report card, actually, that she had had such a great day, Hallie thought as she scribbled on her paper.

Her father had knocked on her door early the next morning, which happened to be a Saturday.

"Get dressed. We're going on a trip," he said.

"Where?" she called, as she rolled over.

"Eugene."

"For what?"

"To celebrate."

"Celebrate what?" she asked, wondering if she had forgotten her father's birthday, or something.

"To celebrate your report card," he said. "Now hurry up. Let's not waste the day."

Hallie got dressed as quickly as she could and rushed down the stairs, but Jane was still wandering around in her bathrobe, and Molly wasn't even up.

She must have looked bewildered for a moment because her father said, "It's just the two of us today, old bean."

"Just you and me, Dad?"

"Yep."

Her father kissed Jane good-bye.

"I haven't eaten breakfast yet."

"Breakfast is part of the prize," her father said, gesturing for her to follow him out of the kitchen.

They stopped in town for breakfast, and her father told her to order anything she wanted, which was a first. He actually never went out for breakfast, though it was something she and her mother loved to do, especially if they were going on a trip.

Hallie ordered a croissant and hot chocolate and a bowl of fruit. Her father ordered oat bran, two pieces of dry toast with jelly on the side, and a cup of herbal tea.

"Sure you want a croissant, Hallie?" he asked before the waitress left the table.

"Yeah, I'm sure."

"I just thought—never mind. You order whatever you like."

"I did," Hallie said, smiling at her father.

"You know, I'm very proud of you," her father said.

"Thanks, Dad."

"I knew you could do it, if you wanted to."

"Yeah," she said, hoping her father didn't expect her to get all A's on every report card.

Hallie smothered her croissant with honey and licked her fingers after she had taken the last bite.

She looked at her father guiltily. He hated it when she did that, but she couldn't resist.

After breakfast they got back into the car and headed toward Eugene.

Her father was just the opposite of her mother. He was very quiet when they were alone in the car. Her mother rarely ever stopped talking. Hallie wasn't sure which was actually better.

"You know, I'm really happy you decided to go to

school here," he said after one of their long silences. "Have I ever told you that?"

"You told me you wanted me to go to school here because it was a better place for me to live."

"Well, I should have told you that I wanted you here for my sake, too," her father said. "And so did Jane."

"Thanks, Dad," Hallie said.

She could have wondered why he was telling her that then, and maybe she did, but as Hallie remembered it now, she felt good about it. Very good, whatever her father's reason was for telling her how he felt.

She hadn't really spent much time in Eugene, so this was such a treat. It was different, very different, from Venice. It had a different feeling to it.

They were lucky that the weather had warmed up for them, so they could walk down the street without freezing to death. When they got too cold to window shop, they'd pop into a bookstore and browse around. There seemed to be a bookstore on every block, which pleased her father no end.

Hallie didn't want to complain because her father had planned such a nice day for her, but she was getting tired of thumbing through magazines and listening to him talk about the real leather covers on some of the books in the used bookstores. But he let her pick out any three books she wanted to buy, and she appreciated that.

They had lunch at a cute little restaurant with checkered cloths and candles on the tables, and a dart board on the wall. There were lots of newspapers and magazines on a wooden bench at the front of the restaurant, and people sat around reading and eating lunch. It was very cozy and friendly. Lots of college students were studying and talking and laughing. Hallie watched them and wondered if she'd ever be as sophisticated as they were.

"Even though I never, never, ever eat red meat, I would really, really, really love to order a hamburger, Dad," Hallie said.

"Like I said, it's your day, Hallie," her father said.

She ordered the hamburger, and he ordered a salad.

After they finished eating Hallie felt stuffed.

"Let's do the secondhand shops," her father said. "Maybe we can pick up something interesting for your room."

It had been a nice, leisurely day. Maybe most kids wouldn't have thought it was fun, but Hallie loved walking in and out of shops with her father, loved looking at all the old clothes and antique jewelry and lamps with leaded glass shades. They bought one for her room. Her father let her pick out the one she liked best.

And just when she thought they would probably be heading home, her father had another surprise for her. They went to see a movie, something she hadn't done since she'd come to Oregon. Then they went to dinner at a fancy restaurant. And she had the best potato-and-leek soup she'd ever tasted.

"Thanks, Daddy. For everything you did for me today," she said when they pulled into their driveway.

She was so tired, she could barely keep her head up and her eyes open, but it was a happy tired, and she meant it. She was grateful to her father. But she was most grateful for the fact that her dad had spent the day—the whole day—with just her. There was something nice about being alone with your father. Something nice about being an only child again.

Chapter Fifteen

It was three-thirty. Hallie was doodling in the margins of her paper. She yawned and stretched. Then she looked at her paper again.

MAPLEWOOD	
Pluses	Minuses
farmhouse	farmhouse
Fuzzy	one TV station
Kate	no movies
school	
Jane	
horseback riding	~~horseback riding~~
basketba	no ballet
barn dance	
being with my dad	

She had made her decision. She didn't need to go on. Clearly, she should return to Oregon for the school year and visit her mother on vacations. She was happy in Oregon. Even though she didn't get to have her father to herself that often, the times she did were really special.

Unconsciously, she erased the little ballet slippers she had drawn and began drawing boxes and shading them in like her father had taught her to do.

Besides, the basketball team needed her. She had friends in Oregon. She had Kate.

Kate was the first person she told when she got her period. She had felt shy about telling anyone, really. She wished more than anything that her mother had been there, even though she knew her mother would make a big deal out of it and embarrass her.

Her mother had prepared her. She'd been preparing her for years, it seemed. Since she first began developing breasts, which she said she hated, though she didn't really. She was more afraid of the changes in her body than anything else. Her mother had told her to be proud of her body, but she still didn't feel comfortable with it, unless she was dancing or playing basketball. But her mother was always talking about becoming a woman, telling her specifically what to do. She had even sent her to Oregon with sanitary pads—just in case. But when her period finally came, it took Hallie by surprise. She'd had a tummy ache in school, but she hadn't thought much about it until she went into the john before basketball practice.

At first she panicked. She wasn't sure the stain on her panties, which had turned a reddish brown, was actually dried blood. And if it was, did that mean she had gotten her period, or was it something else? Some terrible disease, maybe? Because, contrary to what she had always been taught, she never took time to lay those thin tissue covers over toilet seats in public places.

"Hurry up," Kate had yelled to her.

She came out of the toilet stall and walked over to the sink. She stood looking at herself in the mirror. She didn't look any different. Aside from her stomachache, she didn't feel any different. But she had a secret. And somehow she *was* different. She was no longer a girl; she was a young woman.

"You don't have any pimples," Kate said.

"What?"

"Isn't that why you're staring at yourself in the mirror?"

"I got my period," Hallie whispered.

"When?" Kate asked. Her eyebrows were raised, and her eyes twinkled with a kind of mischief that usually spun things around and left Hallie standing in awe of her.

"Just now," Hallie said tentatively.

Like an old pro, Kate walked over to a vending machine on the wall, dropped in two quarters, and retrieved a sanitary pad.

Hallie stood looking at it for a moment.

"Should I show you how to use it?" Kate asked. She laughed as she threw the pad to Hallie.

Hallie could feel herself blushing. "I know how."

"Good. Then hurry up. We're going to be late for practice."

"Is it all right if I play?" Hallie asked.

"Hey, you're just bleeding. You're not dying. It's no big deal."

Yes, it is, Hallie thought. But she didn't say anything.

She simply took the pad and went back into the toilet stall.

She kept the secret to herself that night. She just needed to feel a little more comfortable with it before she told Jane, who took it with the same kind of natural ease Kate did, simply asking her if she had pads.

But when she came home from school, there was a bouquet of flowers in her room with a note from her dad. It didn't mention her period. It just said, "I love you," but she knew that's what it was all about.

Two days later she called her mother.

"Remember when I got my ears pierced?" she asked.

"Sure," Michelle answered.

"Remember how scared I was? And you told me that when Indian girls are old enough to have babies, they go through certain initiations that might be painful. To show they'll be strong enough to bear children when the time comes. And you said that ear piercing was like an initiation. That it might hurt a little, but it was a step toward growing up and being a woman and taking responsibility."

"What made you think about that, Hallie?"

Hallie paused for a minute. "Mommy, guess what? I got my period."

"That's great, Hallie. That's wonderful," her mother gushed. "What did you do to celebrate?"

Hallie rolled her eyes and smiled to herself. "Nothing, Mommy. It's no big deal."

"Of course, it's a big deal. It's a wonderful thing when your body changes. It's important to honor that change."

"Well—remember you said when I got my period,

you'd take me shopping for something very special? Did you mean that?''

''We'll go as soon as you get home,'' her mother said.

And her mother more than kept her promise. They went shopping the day after she came home for spring vacation, and she bought a leather jacket. Real leather.

It eased the pain of having to share her mother with Frank. She had gotten used to having her all to herself since her divorce.

Hallie rifled through her desk, looking for the picture her mother had painted for her to honor her becoming a woman. She had been too embarrassed to show it to any of her friends. They wouldn't have understood, but secretly she had been very pleased. It had made her feel important.

After she had been home for two days, her mother presented her with a wonderful surprise. A trip to Hawaii for just the two of them.

Hallie closed her eyes for a moment as she remembered landing at the airport in Kauai, walking off the plane, feeling as if she were wrapped in a warm blanket of sunshine. The weather in Los Angeles was warm and sunny. But Kauai was hot, and the heat penetrated her whole body.

When Hallie opened her eyes again, she automatically picked up her pencil and placed the California paper on top of the Oregon paper. She would go through the same process and fill out the plus and minus columns after all—just to be fair.

She started to write Hawaii in the plus column, but Hawaii is a place, just like California or Oregon. Did it need a separate column? What should she do? She sat there for a moment, thinking. Maybe Hawaii was more than a place.

As soon as they got settled in their hotel, her mother told her they were going to go to a *heiau*, a sacred place. In Hawaii, a sacred place isn't necessarily a church or synagogue or mosque or temple like it is on the mainland. It could be the side of a rock, or a hilltop, the trunk of a tree. Michelle told Hallie she was going to make an offering to take with her to the *heiau*.

Hallie laughed. "You don't really believe it will do anything, do you, Mommy?"

"I don't know, but we might as well give it a try, Hallie. Come on, walk along the beach with me. I'm going to find some shells and stuff—see what I come up with."

Hallie drove out to Lumahai Beach with her mother. The beach was quiet—and empty. Hallie felt as if they were the first people to stare in awe at the ocean as it spilled over a huge shelf of black rock. The sound of the waves repeatedly crashing onto the shore was hypnotic. And after a few moments Hallie felt as if they were vibrating in her head, traveling across the top of her skull to her forehead.

As they walked along the beach, she felt as if the warm sand was melting under her feet, and, feeling like an intruder who happened upon a sacred ceremony, she stepped gingerly, trying to make herself as light as possible.

Michelle collected an old gourd and some beautiful

shells. Hallie picked up some leaves and shells herself, though she wasn't sure why, or what she was going to do with them.

But, later in their room, while Michelle was gluing her shells onto the gourd, Hallie started gluing together the leaves and shells she had collected together. She created three separate pieces and stood back to look at them. It wasn't that they were so unusual or so beautiful, but for some reason she felt like crying when she looked at them.

Early the next morning, her mother asked, "Are you ready?"

"Sure," Hallie said.

"Take your art objects with you, if you like," Michelle said. "We're going to the *Hula Heiau*."

Hallie started to laugh. "That's pretty funny."

"Yeah, it does sound funny, but it's not really. There's a story that the magic of the hula was revealed to the people of the island by the hula goddess, Laka, on that spot."

"You mean the dance?" Hallie asked, moving her arms languidly, first to the right and then to the left.

"That's just one little part of it. Each tiny movement signifies something. It's like a language of the body. You communicate with your body instead of with words."

"Mommy," Hallie sighed.

"You'll see, Hallie. Or maybe you won't," Michelle said as they got into the car.

They drove to an even more remote part of the coast, parked and hiked down a trail leading to the side of a heavily wooded mountain. Hallie didn't see anything unusual about it, but she decided to just go along with her mother's program.

They climbed up a little way and stopped at a clearing surrounded by rocks and boulders. This was the *Hula Heiau*. Michelle opened her purse and took out a tiny tooth.

"It's your baby tooth," she said to Hallie.

"What are you—"

"I'm going to plant it in this holy spot. It's my way of letting go of my baby."

"Mommy," Hallie said, totally exasperated.

But Michelle either didn't hear her or didn't pay any attention. She knelt down and placed the tooth in a crevice.

Hallie was embarrassed. She saw that other people had left offerings of flowers and fruit. Her mother had brought a tooth.

She didn't really believe in the ritual, she told herself, but she left the three art pieces anyway. And when her mother asked her what they represented to her, she said, "Oh, I don't know. Me and you—and Frank, I guess."

Chapter Sixteen

Hallie sat with her pencil in her mouth, trying to remember everything she could about her trip to Hawaii. Somehow she knew it was important for her to do that. But the seven days they spent there seemed to fuse into one long, sunny afternoon, and she couldn't remember anything else except a lazy kind of warmth creeping through her body and filling her mind with fuzz balls and bougainvillea. It was soothing, comforting, but it was Hawaii. It was a certain state of mind, and it didn't help her with her decision now.

She took her pencil out of her mouth and was about to go on to the next positive or negative point when she suddenly remembered Angelene. Angelene's smooth face and dancing eyes appeared before her, and the whole incredible experience came back to her, filling her mind with vivid images.

Her mother had planned something special for their last day in Kauai, though she didn't really need to. Hallie liked whatever they did together, even when she resisted at first. Sometimes especially when she resisted at first.

"Should I take my bathing suit?" Hallie asked as they headed for the door.

"No, you won't need it," Michelle answered casually.

When they got into the car, her mother said, "I'm taking you for a massage as a way of honoring your menstruation."

"But my leather jacket honored it," Hallie protested.

"That was for your body," Michelle said. "This is for your body and your soul."

"Mommy—"

"Remember when you reminded me about what I said when you got your ears pierced?"

"Yeah."

"Well, this is something like that. An initiation. All initiations are difficult, but they don't have to be terribly difficult. And after you go through them, you feel changed, as if you're really, really ready to go on to the next phase of your life."

Hallie was sorry she'd brought up the earrings.

"I am really, really ready," she said.

"Remember Jason Deutsch had his Bar Mitzvah when he turned thirteen?"

"That was great."

"But he had to study every day after school for weeks in order to prepare for it. And it was difficult, but in the end, I think he felt it was worth it."

"You mean that was like his initiation?"

"Exactly. I think the rabbi even said something about his becoming a man on that day."

"Yeah, but that was kind of funny since he didn't look very much like a man."

"But maybe he felt more grown-up. Maybe he felt as if he could leave some of his baby needs behind."

"Maybe I should have a Bar Mitzvah," Hallie teased, "and a big party to celebrate it."

Michelle laughed. "If we were Jewish, you could have a Bat Mitzvah. *Bat* Mitzvah's are for girls. If we were Japanese, you would learn the tea ceremony. Lots of cultures have ways of celebrating the transition from childhood to adulthood. Unfortunately, most of the ceremonies are for boys.

"In primitive societies, women who were menstruating went to live in special huts, separate from the rest of the community, because they were thought to be so powerful. They fasted and performed other purification rites."

"I don't think I'd be too thrilled about that, Mommy."

"I don't know. Maybe it wasn't such a bad idea. In a way it was similar to the rituals boys experienced before becoming men. It gave women a chance to be alone, get in touch with their souls. Listen to their own voices. But since our society doesn't have any ceremonies or rituals to celebrate the transition from girl to woman, we have to look for our own ways of doing that."

"We don't have to," Hallie insisted. "I'm sure I'll grow up just fine, anyway."

"You'll grow up, anyway," Michelle said. "I grew up, but I didn't grow up just fine."

Hallie was about to ask her mother what she meant when they pulled off onto a long dirt road.

"I'm nervous," she said.

"You don't have to take all your clothes off if you don't want to," her mother assured her.

Instead of reassuring her, Hallie went into shock. She wasn't planning on taking off any of her clothes. She hadn't even thought about that.

Michelle parked the car, and Hallie looked at the large house in front of her that stood alone on a huge plot of land beneath a mountain. She waited for her mother to say something about this being another *heiau*, a holy place, a place of power. But Michelle didn't say anything. Instead she got out of the car, and the two of them walked past the octagonal-shaped house to a smaller one behind it, which stood on stilts.

"We don't get massages right away," her mother explained.

That's good, Hallie thought. It would give her a little more time. Time for what, she wondered.

"We go into the moon lodge first."

"A moon lodge?"

"A sweat."

"A sweat! What is a sweat? And why would I want to do that?"

"Well, well—you'll see. It's hard to explain."

Hallie hung behind her mother as they walked up the stairs and into the house.

Angelene was obviously expecting them. She met them at the door and handed them beautiful, flowered sarongs. "Take off your clothes and wrap these around you," she instructed.

Hallie took the sarong and relaxed a little. At least Angelene didn't expect her to walk around naked.

Then she and her mother both changed and entered the sweat, a small room, very much like a sauna.

"Some people take their sarongs off in the sweat. You can keep yours on if you want to, Hallie," her mother said. "And you don't have to look at anybody else if it makes you uncomfortable."

Hallie kept her sarong on, but after five minutes, the sweat began pouring out of her, and she knew that the room was appropriately named. It was hotter than any sauna she'd ever been in. Not that she'd been in all that many.

She had trouble looking at the women sitting around her in various states of undress. She was the youngest person there by about ten years, she figured, and she was embarrassed by the fat that rolled off some of their bodies. She was even more embarrassed by her own body, which seemed stick-like and boyish.

When her mother took off her sarong, Hallie was surprised that she felt safe enough to reveal her own body, which she professed to believe was ten pounds overweight.

Hallie didn't feel comfortable enough herself to either look at her mother or take off her own sarong, but she found herself beginning to look at the other women. Their bodies, slick and dripping with sweat, began to take on an almost otherworldly appearance. They looked transformed, almost beautiful. Not that their bodies had actually changed. It was something else. Something Hallie couldn't quite understand.

Michelle picked up a small hose and squirted Hallie down. It was a shock to her system, but for a moment, she cooled off. Then she felt as if she were being poached in the water covering her body.

Finally, Angelene said it was her turn for a massage. She was so happy to get out of the sweat that she didn't care what the massage entailed. Let Angelene do whatever it was she did, she was ready.

There were two other women on the massage tables in the next room. One was just lying there with her eyes closed. The other was being worked on by another woman about Angelene's age. While they were in the sweat, her mother had told her that Angelene was in her sixties. But that was hard to believe. She had jet black hair, and her skin was smooth and unlined. There was a certain ageless quality about her, as if she were only about thirty in actual years, but around a hundred in spiritual years, Hallie thought. Then she laughed at herself. She was starting to think like her mother.

Angelene patted the table, and Hallie, still a little self-conscious, surprised herself by slipping out of her sarong and lying face down on the table, without the least bit of resistance.

Angelene began rubbing something that felt like small pebbles into Hallie's body. It felt strange for a moment. Then it began to burn. She murmured.

"It's salts from the sea," Angelene whispered to her.

She rolled sea salt over Hallie's hot, wet skin, and Hallie's body began to awaken. Even though it was a little painful, she felt refreshed, alive.

Then, after the cleansing salt, Angelene rubbed Hallie down with oil, and she began massaging her body with long strokes. With each stroke, Hallie felt as if her body was elongating.

Angelene pushed down and slid her hands from Hallie's neck to her legs in slow, precise movements, and as she massaged Hallie she talked to her in a singsong voice, telling her how beautiful she was. How beautiful her body was.

"You are the first person to celebrate the beginning of her womanhood with us. We are honored. All the women in this room are honored, and we celebrate with you because we did not have the benefit of being celebrated when we reached womanhood. It's very important for you to be here with us today. And it's important for us to have you here. If we can be part of your ceremony, this will be a healing for us, as well."

Angelene motioned for Hallie to turn over, and without a thought about her modesty, Hallie turned and lay on her back. Angelene took her arm and massaged it thoroughly. She pulled it. Then placed it tenderly at her side.

"It's an honor to see a body such as yours," Angelene whispered. "You must accept that honor and honor it yourself."

Hallie felt as if her whole body was singing with Angelene's voice. She felt almost as if she had been reborn. She felt safe and loved and comforted. Most of all she felt totally peaceful. And she wanted to hold on to that feeling forever.

"Now that you are a woman, you have the power to create life," Angelene whispered, "but remember, you also have the power to destroy. Always listen to your body, Hallie. Your body will not lie to you."

Chapter Seventeen

It was four o'clock. Hallie could almost hear the minutes ticking away. In a few hours her mother would be up. In a few hours she would expect to hear Hallie's decision. What should she do? The one thing she did know was that if spring vacation in Hawaii was paradise, having to share her mother with Frank and Dixon was the exact opposite. She wrote "DIXON" under the minus column and underlined it five times.

She had heard about Dixon, of course, but she hadn't really met him until she came home for the summer. Dixon was Frank's son. And to complicate matters, he was the same age as she was—twelve going on thirteen. While Hallie was off in Oregon, Dixon had spent every weekend with his father and her mother. Using her room. Sleeping in her bed.

Just the thought of Dixon made her blood boil.

She had barely gotten off the plane when Dixon arrived. To be fair about it, he was cute enough. But he had the kind of personality only the Terminator could appreciate.

She was sitting there in the living room, minding her own business, just listening to a new tape she had bought in Oregon, when he stumbled in the door with

Frank. Without bothering to pick up his clothes, which had fallen out of his gym bag, he marched right over and switched on the TV.

"This is Dixon," Frank said to her. "Dixon, say hello to Hallie."

Dixon mumbled something, but he didn't bother looking at her, which was just as well because she knew she was sitting there with her mouth open.

Hallie waited for Frank to tell Dixon to pick up all his stuff and turn off the television before her mother came in and had a fit. But he didn't seem to even notice the mess. She stared at him hard, as if she could transmit the message directly into his brain, but Frank said cheerfully, "You two guys get to know each other. I've got some work to do around back before it gets dark."

Hallie turned up the volume on the tape deck and stomped out of the room.

She went into her bedroom, slammed the door behind her, picked up a book from her desk, and sat down on her bed. She couldn't imagine why her heart was beating so fast. It wasn't as if she'd run into her room, and even if she had, it was only a few feet from the living room.

She tried to concentrate on the book. Her breathing became more normal, but she kept reading the same words over and over again.

She was about to get up and go into the kitchen to talk to her mother about this little problem, when Dixon walked right into her room. Without knocking.

"What are you doing?" she asked, trying to control her rage. She knew her voice was shaking, and that made her even madder.

"Looking for my Nintendo game," he said, without looking at her.

"Well, what makes you think it's in here?"

"What makes you think it isn't?" he mumbled.

"There's no reason for your Nintendo game to be in here."

"Is too."

"Is not."

"Is too."

"Oh yeah? What's the reason, then?"

"This is my room when I come here on the weekends," he said stubbornly. "I left it here."

Hallie's eyes opened wide. She was sure she was going to explode.

"Well, it's not your room anymore. On the weekends or any other time. I'm back. This is my room."

"We'll see."

"No, we won't see. I told you, this is my room. It's been my room for the last six years, and it will be my room till the day I die!"

"There's only two bedrooms here," Dixon said anxiously. "Where am I supposed to sleep?"

"How do I know? That's your problem, not mine," Hallie said. Even as she said it, she was aware of how cruel it sounded, but she couldn't seem to stop herself. "Now if you don't mind, would you please leave," she said in a slightly more conciliatory tone of voice.

Instead of leaving, Dixon just stood there as if the wind had been knocked out of him. And instead of feeling sorry for him, it made her even angrier. "Go back to the living room and watch your stupid show," she said. She looked at him and wished him out of her sight and out of her life.

Then she buried her head in her book, dismissing him from the room. She was afraid to look up in case he was still standing there. And in case he could read all the different emotions squeezing their way into her brain, one overlapping the other. Somehow, they all seemed valid. She was proud of herself for standing her ground. At the same time, she was embarrassed for treating Dixon so badly. She knew it wasn't fair for her to expect her mother to close off her bedroom like a shrine waiting for the day when she would occupy it again. But, ~~hell~~, it was *her* room. The least her mother could have done was ask her if it was all right if Dixon used it while she was gone. She wouldn't have liked the idea any more than she did now, but she probably would have agreed to it—reluctantly.

She threw the book down on the bed. She was angry. Angry with everyone. But some part of her knew that the anger was just masking her real emotion. She was hurt and upset. And scared, too, she realized now. It was as if part of her had been violated. Dixon had occupied her private world, the world that had always been just hers. All she had to do was close the door behind her. That was the rule. If she didn't want anyone to come into her room, she could just say so, and both her parents respected that. Now someone had not only come in without her permission, he had slept in her bed.

She could feel the tears well up in her eyes. Before she had a chance to get really maudlin, however, her anxiety clicked into gear again, and she jumped off her bed and headed for the kitchen. He'd made one good point. Where *was* he going to sleep?

As she hurried through the living room, she heard Frank consoling Dixon, who was, she thought, crying.

"You will have a place to stay, Dixon. Michelle put a futon in her studio for you."

"Outside?" he whined.

"It's right next to the house, and—"

Hallie was so relieved, she felt almost lighthearted. Dixon couldn't really have been crying. It had obviously been her imagination. What was there to cry about anyway? It wasn't as if this was really his house. He had a room of his own in some big house in Malibu where he really lived.

"Want me to set the table?" she asked her mother as she all but bounced into the kitchen.

"Sure," Michelle said. "Did you meet Dixon?"

"Yeah, sort of."

"He's a nice boy."

"I guess," Hallie said.

"He is," her mother said, and she winked at Hallie, as if she could read her mind. "Put soup spoons on the table, too, will you?"

Dinner was slightly more pleasant. It was as if Dixon were a completely different person around her mother. No wonder she thought he was a nice boy.

"May I please have another bowl of soup, Michelle?" he asked with a smile. "I really like this, Dad."

Hallie was going to say the same thing, but once Dixon said it, it didn't seem worthwhile.

"Isn't this nice?" Michelle said when they were eating dessert. "It's so good to have Hallie home."

"For the summer," Dixon added.

"Did you bring your books with you?" Frank asked.

"Forgot," Dixon said.

Hallie could tell by the expression on his face that he was lying. But Frank didn't call him on it.

"You've got to do well in summer school, son," Frank said. "Or you'll have to—"

"I know, Dad."

"If you remember to bring your English book next time, maybe Hallie can help you," Michelle said.

"Mommy—"

"Or your dad."

"Sure. Maybe we could do some of the work together," Frank said, halfheartedly.

Of course, Dixon never did remember to bring his English book the entire summer. He said he'd either lost it, or forgotten it, or left it in his mother's car. Pretty soon, Frank stopped asking him if he'd brought it.

Hallie had never seen anyone watch so much television in her whole life. Even she got bored with it after a while, though she thought that's all she would want to do once she got back to California.

When Michelle reminded Frank to find out how Dixon was doing in his summer school class, Frank said that was his mother's responsibility. Hallie couldn't believe that he didn't even seem to care whether Dixon passed the course, or not. And neither did Dixon. She asked him about it once herself, but he just said he didn't feel like doing any work on the weekend. So basically, Dixon came over every weekend and watched TV and fought with Hallie when no one was around.

Whenever any adults were present, however, Dixon was the picture of perfection. He was so polite to everyone, it about turned Hallie's stomach. All her mother's friends told her how sweet he was. Saccharine was more like it, Hallie thought. But everyone bought into it. And Frank praised every little thing he did that was the least bit positive.

One day she helped her mother make a really special dinner. They planned it all out together. And it wasn't even anybody's birthday. But her mother could find a reason to celebrate just about anything if she wanted to.

"It's the summer solstice," she said. "We have to celebrate the change of seasons."

This, of course, was pretty funny, since there are no change of seasons in southern California. It's pretty much summer all year round, give or take ten degrees one way or the other. But Hallie went along with her mother and even got into the spirit of it. They worked for hours. It was really kind of fun, though cooking wasn't something she was all that interested in.

Frank and Dixon had had some kind of argument before they came to the table, Hallie was sure. They were very polite to each other, but neither of them looked at the other. Her mother must have thought so, too. She was more cheerful and funny than usual and didn't analyze anything, didn't give any lectures on the solstice, just made everyone feel better.

After dinner Dixon cleared the table, and Frank said at least five times, "Dixon cleaned up after dinner all by himself."

Well, whoopie. Give the guy a medal, why don't you? He never even mentioned the fact that she had slaved away in the kitchen all day.

Chapter Eighteen

It was four-thirty. Hallie was beginning to panic. But as she sat thinking about Dixon, she remembered another night when she couldn't sleep. She remembered lying in bed listening to her mother and Frank talking.

It had been one of those days where everything seemed to go wrong. Frank had gone to pick up Dixon, as usual, on Friday afternoon, but Dixon wasn't at his house. So Frank had come back feeling annoyed with both Dixon and Marian, his ex-wife.

Michelle was lying down.

Frank came stomping into the house, barely noticing Hallie, and threw his keys down on the table. "Michelle," he called out, and without waiting for her to answer, he headed for their bedroom.

"You know if Dixon doesn't want to come here, the least Marian could do is call and let me know before I drive all the way to Malibu to get him."

Her mother sighed heavily. Frank obviously didn't notice.

"Last weekend he said he was bored. There's nothing to do. He has no friends here."

"I haven't been feeling well all day," Michelle murmured.

"I've asked him to help me with the work around the house, but he's not interested in that."

"You and Hallie will have to do dinner, Frank."

"All he does is sit in front of the TV set the whole time he's here."

"I really don't feel well."

"I feel like a workhorse. Strap on the harness and I plow the fields for somebody else's benefit. If only I didn't have such high alimony payments. I—"

"I know. It just isn't fair," Michelle said.

At this point, Hallie figured the best thing she could do would be to disappear. She was about to go into her room when the phone rang. She ran into the kitchen to answer it. It was Marian.

Hallie called to Frank and held the phone to her ear, expecting to hear him pick up the extension in the bedroom. Instead he came into the kitchen, looking as if he had totally wilted. He took the phone from her. She walked into the living room and headed toward her bedroom, but, curious about what had happened to Dixon, she stopped for a moment to listen. And because the house was so small, she could hear Frank's side of the conversation very clearly.

"I did come for him," she heard Frank say.

"No, he wasn't there. I came about four-thirty." There was a pause, then he repeated, "Four-thirty."

Frank usually spoke very softly. He was still speaking softly, but Hallie could sense his frustration escalating.

"You want me to drive all the way out there again? Now?"

She heard Frank sigh deeply.

"Then why don't you drop him off on your way?" he asked.

There was a long pause. Hallie wasn't sure if he was still on the phone. She strained to listen.

"Does that mean he failed the whole summer school session?" he said finally.

Hallie turned back toward the kitchen, so she could hear better.

"I would have, if you had made sure he had his books when he came here."

Ha, Hallie thought. That's what happens when you never do your work. What did he expect? What did any of them expect? If they'd have asked her, she could have told them this would happen. But nobody asked her.

"Well, somebody has to take responsibility," Frank said.

She heard Frank hang up the phone. He let out another sigh and walked back through the living room to the bedroom.

"I have to go back to Malibu for Dixon," he told her mother.

"Can't he skip one weekend?"

"No."

"Then why wasn't he there when you went for him?"

"I don't know, Michelle. He just wasn't."

"I really don't feel well enough to have him here this weekend."

"Well, his mother doesn't want him either," Frank said. "It seems as if she's made other plans, and she doesn't want to leave Dixon in the house alone."

"He's almost thirteen."

"He doesn't like to stay there by himself."

"Frank—"

"I'm sorry. What do you want me to do?"

"Just tell him—"

"You tell him. Where's the phone? Why can't I ever find anything around here?"

"Never mind," her mother said. Then she started to cry. "Sometimes I just feel so overwhelmed."

Hallie heard Frank comfort her mother, tell her everything was going to be all right. She'd feel better tomorrow. He'd handle everything.

"Why don't you just try to take a little nap while I'm gone? I'll stop and get some Chinese food on the way home," he said.

Her mother stopped crying. Frank came out of the bedroom and walked into the living room. He just stood in the middle of the room for a minute, as if he were trying to remember exactly what he was doing. Then he said, more to himself than to Hallie, she was sure, "I'm too old to have a thirteen-year-old son. I'm too old, and I hate baseball, and I've never been fishing in my life. All I know how to do is build things. That's all I know. I'm not a psychologist, am I?"

He picked up his keys and walked out the door without waiting for an answer.

The Chinese food was cold, of course, and they forgot to put the rice in, so everyone complained loudly. Frank even called the restaurant and told them how upset he was. At least he tried. It wasn't at all clear whether they understood him, and he was more frustrated than ever when he hung up the phone.

"That was all I was going to eat," her mother said. "Rice and tea. That's all I felt like having."

"Hallie, go see if there's any rice in the cupboard," Frank said. "I'll make you some, Michelle."

Hallie looked, but she didn't see any.

"I'm sure there's rice," Michelle said. "You're just not looking in the right place."

"I'm looking in the right place," Hallie said. "There's no rice."

Frank walked over to the cupboard, as if he didn't believe her. He scanned the shelves for a moment and pulled out a box of rice.

"Well, it wasn't there before," Hallie said.

"Right," Dixon said.

"What do you know?" Hallie snapped back.

"That's enough," Frank said.

"I'll make it," Hallie said. She grabbed the box from Frank and walked over to the stove.

They ate their dinner, such as it was, in silence, except when someone asked for something to be passed.

After dinner, her mother went back into her room, followed by Frank. Hallie and Dixon argued about who was going to clean the pot she'd used to make the rice, some of which had stuck to the bottom of it. Then they argued about which television program to watch. Dixon won, as usual, because by the time they sat down in the living room, Hallie was tired of fighting. She actually didn't like to fight. It made her uncomfortable. She didn't like to hear other people fighting, either. That made her more than uncomfortable. It scared her. Which was why she remembered that night so clearly.

It was late. Dixon had gone into the studio to sleep, and she had said good-night to her mother and Frank hours ago. But the day lay so heavily on her that she couldn't fall asleep. Her eyes were closed, and she tried to talk herself into it, but sleep kept eluding her.

That's when she heard them whispering about her and Dixon.

"Hallie doesn't do anything around the house," Frank said. "She watches way too much TV."

Hallie sat up in bed. She couldn't stand it when anyone said anything negative about her. Especially when it wasn't even true.

"Hallie's not the problem," her mother countered. "Dixon is."

"Dixon doesn't have all the advantages Hallie has," Frank said. "I think Hallie should be a little more sensitive to that."

Hallie balked. She wasn't the one who was insensitive.

"Doesn't have the advantages?" her mother whispered. "He's the one who lives in a big house in Malibu."

"That's not what I mean, and since when does that kind of thing impress you, anyway?"

"Well, it doesn't. I was just—"

"You know Dixon has a learning disability."

Yeah, Hallie thought, he sure does. He can't even remember to bring his books over.

"Well, maybe if you spent some time working with him instead of just asking him if he's done the work, it might help a little," her mother said, exasperated.

"How can I work with him if he doesn't bring his books?" Frank asked, even more exasperated than her mother.

There was a long silence. Hallie wasn't sure what was going on. She was about to lie down again when her mother answered Frank. "That's not the problem,

Frank,'' she said so softly that Hallie could barely hear her. ''The real problem is that he's invading our space.''

Hallie gasped. For some reason her mother's words felt like a punch in the stomach.

''I know it's mean, but I hate it when he comes and stays in my studio. That's where I create. There's stuff in the air, and he disturbs it.''

''Stuff?''

''Yeah, stuff. Things you can't explain or define. And when I come in there, and Dixon's things are all over the place, it puts me off. I don't feel like it's my place anymore. His shoes are in the middle of the floor. His games are on my desk. The sheets and covers are all over the place. It changes the atmosphere.''

By the next day Michelle, still a little drawn, was obviously feeling better, but Hallie couldn't quite forget the conversation she'd overheard the night before. And she couldn't ignore her own feelings toward Dixon, who was off on an errand with Frank. So after she'd taken her mother's emotional temperature and decided she was cool, Hallie took a chance and told her how she felt.

''It's just that he's so—so whiny,'' she said. ''It really bugs me.''

She expected her mother to agree with her, given the feelings she'd expressed the night before, but Michelle had either forgotten what she'd said or didn't seem to be as bothered this morning. To Hallie's surprise, she came to Dixon's defense.

''Hallie, you've been an only child for a long time, and I'm sure it's hard to get used to having a stepbrother around.''

"Stepbrother?" The very thought of Dixon as a relative made her ill.

"Of course. What did you think he was?"

"Well, just Dixon, I guess."

"Well, since Frank is my husband, and Dixon is his son, he is your stepbrother."

Hallie hadn't thought of Dixon in those terms before, but it didn't make her feel any better about him.

"He always has the TV on. He gets on my nerves," she said, hoping her mother would see where she was leading and tell her what she had told Frank.

"Listen, honey, I understand your point of view. And maybe we ought to make a rule that two hours of television a day is enough, but you've got to understand— Dixon has some problems."

"I know Mommy, that's what I'm trying to tell you."

"I mean he doesn't always feel really good about himself."

"Well, Frank comes to his defense no matter what he does. He never tells him he's doing anything wrong. And whenever he does the slightest positive thing, Frank thinks he's so wonderful. Everyone thinks he's so nice. All the adults. He's not nice to me."

"Maybe he's jealous of you."

"Of me?" Hallie said, shocked.

"Of course."

"Why me?"

"Think about it, Hallie. Just think about it, okay?"

"Do I have to?"

"You have to—if you want to."

"Thanks a lot, Mom," Hallie said, as she walked rigidly out of the room.

"You're welcome," her mother called after her.

Chapter Nineteen

Five o'clock. The rest of the house was silent, but the kitchen clock was ticking away as Hallie walked in to get a glass of water. If only she had someone neutral to talk to. Someone who could help her figure out what to do. She was sure her mother wanted her to stay in California. She didn't really put any outward pressure on her, but there was an unspoken contract between them, and in the small print it stated that mothers and daughters are *supposed* to be together. That's just the way it was. Unless, of course, there was some terrible reason not to be. Like if your mother was a criminal, which her mother wasn't. Or if your mother just couldn't take care of you, which her mother could. At least most of the time.

Of course, her father would be very disappointed if she didn't come back to Oregon. He clearly wanted her there. He really believed it was the best place for her to grow up. And maybe it was. She loved the freedom, the space. She'd fallen in love with her baby half sister Molly, who was so adorable. Hallie sighed. She loved lots of things about Oregon. Just as she loved lots of things about Venice.

What should she do? She knew that no matter what

she said, her mother would feel rejected if she went back to Oregon, and her father would feel rejected if she stayed in California. She glanced at the clock and panicked. Time was running out on her, and she had no better idea now than she had had hours ago.

She wished she could call Kate, but it was the middle of the night. She filled her glass and carried it back to her room. Her mother allowed her to call every other week, and Kate called her sometimes, too. They talked until either her mother or Kate's yelled for them to get off the phone.

Hallie had called earlier in the week, but Kate wasn't home, and she hadn't returned the call. The last time they talked, Kate told her she had gone horseback riding with Peter. Peter! Why would Kate be wasting her time on someone she usually tried to avoid? When Hallie had asked her why, Kate just laughed and changed the subject.

Despite her panic—maybe because of it—Hallie let her mind wander again. She could see Kate's face in front of her. Her red hair, her smile, her eyes that always seemed to see more than anyone else's. She could see Kate riding against the wind, her hair whipping through the air. She could see her standing at her locker and waiting at the bus stop. She could see her at the barn dance at her house. The image of Kate was so clear in her mind's eye that Hallie felt as if she could reach out and touch her red plaid shirt.

Just before Hallie came home for the summer, she and Jane and her father had swept the inside of their old barn clean and painted it. All the leaks in the roof were patched up, and two coats of red paint were applied to the exterior. They hauled in bales of hay, hung lanterns, put straw in the loft, went to yard sales and found old wagon wheels, and really fixed the place up. It looked great.

"We did it," her father said, as he finished the final touch-up work and put his paintbrush down.

Hallie was limp with exhaustion, but she could feel a grin sneaking across her face.

"We wouldn't have gotten around to doing this for years if it hadn't been for you, Hallie," Jane said. Jane was lugging an old milk can she'd bought at auction into the barn. Molly was strapped to her back like a papoose. The three of them stood back and examined their work. Everything looked so authentic, her father said they should buy a horse next.

After they cleaned out the brushes, they walked back to the house. Jane took Hallie's hand and gave it a squeeze. Hallie could still remember how it felt. It was meant to be more than just a squeeze. Hallie knew that and squeezed back.

After all their work, she was afraid that no one would come to their barn dance. The day of the party, she was so nervous. Every hour she counted the hours until she could expect the first guest. She ran up and down the stairs, checking out her clothes, straightening up the house, washing her hair.

She called Kate twice. Kate assured her she was coming. Juneann was coming. Everyone she knew was coming. And Kate was right. They did come. Everyone from school came, and the people with whom her father and Jane had become friendly. The barn shook with music and dancing. The food was gobbled up, and no one went home until after midnight.

Hallie was so excited at the time, faces just whizzed past her. She talked to lots of people, helped Jane and her father serve the food, danced, and worried about whether everyone was having a good time. So, though she saw all her friends and acquaintances, she concentrated on no one, and it wasn't until this minute that she realized Kate and Peter had been partners the whole evening, just as they had at Juneann's. Then she realized that Peter had attended every one of their basketball games. Lots of other people had, too, but now she knew instinctively that Peter had been there to see Kate.

And it finally hit her. They liked each other. They liked each other a lot. They always had.

Now that she had spent some time away from Kate, she understood her better. And she was beginning to understand something about friendships with the opposite sex. There seemed to be a sort of combative element in male-female relationships. It was that way with her parents. With Jane and her father sometimes. With her mother and Frank. With Kate and Peter. Maybe that's why people said "the opposite sex." Like the opposite team. It was almost as if there was some kind of edge that was somehow different from the excitement she felt when she was with a girlfriend she loved. It was almost as if there was a tension of sorts between men and women. Not exactly a bad tension. But a tension that sometimes kept people away from each other, almost as if they were afraid it would get out of hand. Sometimes it did. Like with her mother and father.

She missed Kate. She missed her a lot. That was a

good reason to go back to Oregon. She wanted to sit on her bed and listen to music and talk to her and laugh, and tell her she knew Kate liked Peter.

Hallie put her glass of water down on the desk. But if she went back, she would miss Chloe. And Chloe had become her friend here.

She picked up her pencil and wrote "Chloe" under the plus column, because Chloe was a plus in her life. A very important plus. She was totally different from Kate, but Hallie liked being with her just as much as she liked being with Kate. Maybe more.

Hallie met Chloe the same day she moved into the neighborhood with her family. Chloe had never lived on a walk street before, and that's all she could talk about for a while. Hallie had lived on their walk street practically all her life and didn't realize how unusual it was until she listened to Chloe going on and on about it.

"Don't you love that there's just a sidewalk between my house and your house?" Chloe asked. "Don't you just love that no cars can drive down our street?"

"Yeah, it's neat," Hallie answered, and suddenly it had seemed neat that the only access to their houses by car was the alley behind them.

It would take someone like Chloe to point that out, Hallie thought. Or like Kate. Kate would have mentioned it right away, too. Kate took everything in, and Chloe didn't take anything for granted. Probably because of the way she was brought up. Every morning she and her family prayed for strength to do the best they could that day and be the best they could be, and every evening they thanked God for allowing them to live in such a wonderful place and eat well and prosper. At first Hallie was kind of embarrassed by all the praying. But when she got to thinking about it, she decided it actually was kind of nice. Sometimes when she woke up, she pretended she was at Chloe's house and prayed the same little prayer they did, and the funny thing was that she usually danced better at her dance classes on those days, though some part of her couldn't really believe that it had anything to do with the prayer.

Chloe's father was a doctor and her mother was a teacher. Both parents were very religious and very strict. In fact, Chloe wasn't allowed to visit Hallie, even though they lived a few doors away from each other, until her parents met Michelle. Hallie was afraid that might blow the friendship, but her mother really came through and invited Chloe's parents for tea and didn't talk about Ereshkigal. And Frank didn't come dancing into the room in one of his wild shirts and ruin everything, so Chloe's parents said it would be fine if they were friends.

Hallie had had a few other friends who were African-American, but none of them had actually come from Africa like Chloe and her family. They had moved to the Untied States from Nigeria three years ago. And everything they did seemed very exotic and exciting to Hallie. The way they looked. The way they spoke. The way they dressed, the food they ate, their good manners and extreme politeness.

Hallie's family was Christian. More or less. They went to church on Christmas and Easter. Sometimes. But her mother said that Christianity didn't really fill her needs anymore. She was more interested in pre–Judeo-Christian religions where people worshipped earth goddesses. But Hallie was free to make her own decisions, and if she wanted to go to church with Chloe's family, that was certainly fine with her. In fact, her mother thought it would be an incredible experience.

And it was. Going to church with Chloe's family was not like going to any church she had ever been to before.

Early Sunday morning they all piled into the Agake's old station wagon. Chloe, her parents, her older brother Chenua and Chenua's friend, Robert.

Everyone sat stiffly, looking straight ahead as if they all had to keep their eyes on the road in order to assist Dr. Agake. Hallie squirmed uncomfortably in a dress she hadn't worn for over a year. It was too small for her, but no one seemed to notice except Robert, who kept glancing at her out of the corner of his eye.

Hallie was surprised when Dr. Agake pulled onto the freeway. She was even more surprised when he headed downtown and got off in an area totally unfamiliar to her.

When they got out of the car and headed across the parking lot, Hallie noticed other families getting out of their cars. They were all black. She and Robert were the only light-skinned people. For a moment Hallie imagined that everyone was staring at them hostilely, but as they entered the church, people smiled and greeted her and Robert as if they were part of the family.

They filed into a pew, and Hallie found herself sitting between Chloe and Robert. When she and Robert reached for a prayer book at the same time, their hands touched accidentally, and they both pulled back as if they had been stung by a bee.

"Go ahead," Robert said.

"That's okay," Hallie said, almost afraid to reach for the book again.

Robert was about to say something else, but Chloe leaned over and whispered in her ear that some girls from her old school had just come in.

"They're mean," Chloe said.

"How come?" Hallie whispered back.

"Just best to stay out of their way."

Before she could ask why, the choir filed in and stood quietly behind the pulpit. A hush came over the congregation. The choirmaster raised his arms, and suddenly music swelled out of the choir and filled the church. "Holy, holy," they sang. "Oh holy, holy." Then this incredible soprano voice rose above the rest of the choir, sending chills through Hallie, and she felt just as she had when she was standing on the beach in Hawaii.

"Ah-men," someone in the congregation shouted as the song ended.

"Ah-men," the rest of the congregation echoed.

"Ah-ah-men," the choir sang.

"Amen," Hallie said under her breath. Then the choir burst into another song. People around her started clapping. Some of the members of the choir started clapping and swaying, and pretty soon the whole building was alive with humming and singing. And people in the congregation in their fine dresses and suits with ties were standing up, eyes closed, swaying to the music, shouting, "Ah-huh. You got it. That's right." And

Hallie wanted desperately to jump up and shout right along with them, but she was too embarrassed.

"I love this African music," she whispered to Chloe.

Chloe laughed. "It's American music. Gospel. We're probably the only African family here."

Hallie had never sat in church for so many hours, but it wasn't boring. Though she couldn't remember much of anything the minister said. She loved the way he said, "Je-sus," with the accent on the last vowel. He almost sang it. This was nothing like the churches she had gone to before where everyone sat quietly, listening to the minister, singing softly with the choir, bored to death. No one was bored at Chloe's church. And everyone was very nice to her. Just about everyone.

After the service, the girls from Chloe's old school swaggered over to them. One of the girls lit into to Chloe, just loud enough for Hallie to hear. "Why you with that white girl? Don't you know any better?" she said.

Hallie stood frozen. For a moment she wondered if Chloe was going to tell her she'd made a mistake. She couldn't be her friend. After all, Chloe was like her. She hated confrontation. But Chloe just smiled and said, "I don't pick my friends because of their color. You want to be friends with me, that's fine, but I'm going to be friends with Hallie, too. Hear?"

"Well excuse me," the other girl said, and she ran off laughing.

Hallie started to thank Chloe for her support, but Chloe just shrugged her shoulders and said, "I don't listen to stupid talk like that. I can pick anyone I want for a friend. Always have and always will."

* * *

When they finally got back from church, it was almost two o'clock. They sat down to a huge lunch. Dr. Agake at the head of the table, Mrs. Agake at the foot, and the four kids in between. Girls on one side, boys on the other. Hallie was about to pick up her fork, when Robert kicked her under the table. She thought it was an accident until Mrs. Agake bowed her head and said, "We thank You, God, for letting Hallie and Robert join us today. We thank You for the beautiful day, and for this precious food." "Amen," everyone else said. Hallie said, "Amen" after them, and she meant it.

If I do go back to Oregon, maybe Chloe can come visit me, Hallie thought. She drew a smiley face on the paper, but suddenly she didn't feel like smiling. Her back began to ache from sitting in one place for so long. Her hands felt dry. Her head began to hurt, and it wasn't just because it was so late, and she was tired. Her body was talking to her. Maybe it was telling her something she really didn't want to hear.

"Listen to your body, Hallie," Angelene had said.

Well, she was listening. She was being forced to listen, whether she wanted to or not, but she couldn't understand what her body was saying. Maybe she didn't want to. It pained her to acknowledge the fact that her good friend—maybe her best friend—would not be welcome in Oregon.

Chapter Twenty

Hallie and Chloe sat on a bench, their ballet slippers on the floor beside them. The other girls in the class had already changed into their tennis shoes and were on their way, but Michelle had said she might be a few minutes late today, so they took their time getting back into their civilian clothes.

"That was really a workout," Chloe said.

"I'm exhausted," Hallie said, leaning back against the wall. She loved going to summer dance classes with her friend. She knew some of the other kids from past summers, but she hadn't seen them for a long time, since she had attended dance camp in Colorado last summer.

When Chloe heard about dance camp, she begged her mother to let her go, too. She had taken ballet classes before she moved to Venice, and she and Hallie realized, to their delight, they were at about the same place.

Chloe's mother and father discussed it for three days nonstop, interviewed Michelle, and finally agreed to let her attend. The only problem was there was no room. Both girls were crushed.

Then Michelle had an idea. She called the head of the camp and talked him into it, telling him Chloe was a very talented dancer, and he would really be missing out on something if he couldn't find a spot for her.

When Hallie overheard the conversation, she was elated. She stood listening to Michelle, and then she began jumping up and down, clapping her hands together softly, whispering, "Yes. Yes."

But as soon as her mother hung up the phone and smiled, saying that Chloe was in, Hallie also felt something else. She felt slightly—very slightly jealous. She was proud of her friend. She was proud of her mother for going to bat for her. But she also felt kind of strange listening to her mother talk about another girl that way. That was the way Michelle talked about her—Hallie. She wasn't sure she liked hearing her say she thought someone else was special. Even Chloe.

But almost as soon as she acknowledged the feeling, she shoved it down—way down—inside of her, willing it to go away immediately. And it disappeared, just like that, as if she'd never thought it.

Occasionally, the green monster tried to crawl out of her stomach and gnaw at her—like today when Pierre, their dance instructor, singled Chloe out for praise. The monster surprised her by jumping right into her ear and whispering, "Your mother never should have pressured Craig to let Chloe into the class."

She disowned the monster immediately, of course. The real Hallie would never have allowed such a thought to enter her mind. At least, that's what she liked to tell herself, even if she didn't quite believe it. Maybe the green monster was Ereshkigal. Maybe everybody had an Ereshkigal inside of them. She looked at Chloe out of the corner of her eye and wondered if Chloe knew what she was thinking.

They were tying up their laces when Michelle beeped the horn for them. They stuffed their leotards into their gym bags, picked the bags up, and ran out to the car.

"Only one more week of camp this session," Chloe said.

"Yeah, but we have three more weeks of the short session after that," Hallie reminded her.

"Then there's only one week till school," Chloe said. "That makes me really nervous."

"How come?"

"It's a new school. I won't know anybody, except you."

Hallie swallowed hard. "I'm not going to school here, Chloe," she said.

"Why?" Chloe almost shouted from the backseat of the car.

"I went to school in Oregon last year, and—"

"You never told me," Chloe said accusingly.

"I must have."

"You didn't. I'm sure."

"But I must have."

"I would have remembered. I thought—" Chloe's voice trailed off to an obviously disappointed murmur.

"But you'll make friends," Hallie assured her. She was going to say something else, but her voice unexpectedly caught in her throat.

"There's a new magnet school starting in our area," Chloe said in a flat voice. "My parents were going to talk to your mother about it."

"What kind of magnet?" Michelle asked, joining the conversation.

"An environmental school. My dad heard about it at

the hospital. The son of one of the other doctors is going there. There's regular classes, but there are also classes in environmental studies. My dad thinks that's very important.''

"He's right," Michelle said. "After all, we only have one planet, and we sure don't respect it very much.''

"My dad said if we don't learn to respect the earth and the atmosphere, we'll have to pay the consequences," Chloe said.

"We're already paying," Michelle said. "We can't even swim in the ocean around here anymore. We're a twenty-minute walk to the beach, but the water's not safe to swim in. It's pathetic.''

They all heaved a collective sigh.

"Only I wish Hallie was going to school here," Chloe said.

"Me too," Michelle said.

Hallie felt a lump in her throat. It began to swell up. She looked out the window and kept looking until her mother pulled into the garage.

She wasn't going to ask Chloe if she wanted to come in, as she usually did when they got home from dance camp. She didn't much feel like it today. But Chloe just kind of followed her into the house anyway.

"You know that movement we learned at the end of the session?" Chloe asked.

"Yeah," Hallie murmured.

"I don't think I quite got it. Would you go over it with me?"

"I thought you were exhausted.''

"If you're too tired—''

"That's okay.''

"We could do it tomorrow.''

"Never mind," Hallie said. She kicked off her shoes without unlacing them, then she slipped in a CD and got into position.

Chloe moved over next to her, watching her carefully.

"And one and two and—" Hallie said. She swept her hands out in front of her and raised her left leg so that it was parallel to the ground. Despite being tired, all the tension left her body, and she felt as if she were being miraculously lifted into the air by some unseen partner.

"Again," Chloe said. "I think I'm getting it."

Hallie repeated the movement, and lost in her body, she didn't hear the door open. She didn't see Dixon come into the house. She didn't hear Frank drive off to do some errand. She wasn't aware of anything except the buzz of freedom inside of her.

Until the television blared, scaring her back to reality.

She stopped dancing. Chloe stopped dancing. They both stood glaring at Dixon.

"What are you looking at?" he asked, sneering at them.

Chloe was too polite to answer.

"You," Hallie said, angrily.

"I watch this program every Friday," Dixon said turning up the volume even louder. He turned around and looked straight at Chloe. "And if you don't like it, you know what you can do."

"I better go," Chloe said, as she inched toward the door.

"Chloe—" Hallie begged.

"See you later."

Chloe opened the door and ran out, leaving her shoes behind.

"Chloe," Hallie yelled, as she ran past Dixon, almost tripping over him.

"Why do you have to be so rude?" she asked, exasperated.

Dixon shrugged his shoulders as Hallie picked up her own shoes and marched into her bedroom with them. She slammed the door shut, slumped down on her bed, and began untying the laces. She would put her shoes on and go right over to Chloe's to apologize for Dixon's behavior, she decided. But before she had a chance to retie them, someone knocked on her door.

"Who is it?" she growled.

"Chloe."

Hallie ran to the door and opened it.

"I'm sorry," they both said at the same time.

Slightly bewildered, they looked at each other for a moment, then once again at the same time, both said, "You're sorry?"

They started to giggle, and the tension dissipated.

"You first," Hallie said.

The two girls sat with their legs crossed in front of them, Buddha-like, in the middle of Hallie's bed.

"I—I shouldn't have run out on you like that," Chloe said.

"I was about to run out myself," Hallie assured her. "I swear, sometimes he makes me want to scream."

"I know," Chloe said. "That's why I should have stayed. If you can't be there to back up a friend, then you're not much of a friend, are you?"

"But you are my friend. You stood up for me when those girls at your church—"

"That was different. This is your house—and Dixon's, sort of. The church belongs to everybody. I—I felt so horrible. Like I wasn't wanted. Like he just wanted me to disappear."

"He did," Hallie said. "And you did."

"Yeah, but then as soon as I got home, I thought, so what if Dixon made me feel bad, he makes you feel a lot worse. So here I am."

Hallie reached over and hugged Chloe.

"But why did *you* say you were sorry?" Chloe asked.

"Just sorry about what happened," Hallie said, "but really, really glad you cared enough to come back, even though you didn't have to."

"Yeah, but I did have to."

"Thanks."

"I gotta go help my mom with dinner," Chloe said, as she got up from the bed.

"Chloe—"

"Yeah?"

"Today in dance class—"

"Yeah?"

"You looked great."

"So did you."

"I was jealous."

"But—"

"It's okay. I don't feel that way anymore."

Chloe smiled at her as she opened the bedroom door. "By the way," she said, "Robert said to say hi to you."

"Robert?"

"You know, my brother's friend."

"I know. He said to say hi to me?"

"He was at our house when I got home."

"He said me in particular?"

"He likes you, Hallie."

Hallie blushed. "If he's still there when you get back, tell him I said hi."

Chapter Twenty-one

As long as she was halfway out the door of her bedroom, Hallie figured she might as well go into the living room and retrieve her ballet slippers. As she picked them up, Dixon mumbled something unintelligible. She should have just ignored him, but she was feeling good, so she thought she'd give him another chance. Maybe he was trying to apologize.

"What?" she asked.

" 'Tell Robert I said hi,' " he said, mimicking her.

Hallie was about to throw her ballet slippers at him when she noticed her skateboard leaning against the wall.

She dropped the slippers, picked up her skateboard, and without a word to anyone, ran out of the house and shoved off toward the beach.

She skated down the walk streets to Palms, then she veered around Windward Circle, past the post office, to the boardwalk. The sun was going down, and the beach was almost deserted. Vendors were closing up their sidewalk shops, boxing their merchandise, and packing it into their vans to store it overnight.

As she skated by, watching them out of the corner of her eye, the combination of the sun's setting and the colorful T-shirts and workout pants, toys, and sunglasses being· swept up and out of sight, made it seem as if all the color was fading from the earth.

But when she got to Rose Avenue, the sun was sinking into the ocean, spreading reddish colors onto the sand and gold streaks across the sky and into the water. Hallie stopped to watch. It almost took her breath away.

On the other side of the boardwalk, across from the ocean, a full moon was rising over the low buildings. She felt caught between beginnings and endings. It made her feel a little sad, despite the beauty. Perhaps because no matter how badly she wanted to hold onto the moment, it kept changing.

She picked up her skateboard and began walking slowly, reluctant to leave, just as two homeless men were approaching her.

"Got any change?" one of them asked.

She shook her head no. Then she shivered. As soon as the sun went down, it got cold at the beach.

She had also been warned, more than once, not to hang around there after dark. It wasn't safe. But she had been away so long, she had forgotten that she had to worry about such things in the city.

The beach, filled with tourists and natives during the day, was deserted at night. It was left to the street people who had nowhere else to go and druggies who had usurped the boardwalk and made it their turf.

Hallie looked around anxiously. A tall, thin guy was heading toward her, his head nodding as if he were listening to his own private music. He raised his hand in some kind of salute, but she didn't wait to see what he wanted. She hopped back on her skateboard and headed back to her house in record time, working up a terrific sweat.

When she could see her house, she slowed down. Her mother was out front calling her name. Frank was heading down the street toward her. "Hallie," he called out. "Is that you?"

The walk streets were dark, and it was hard to see.

"Yeah," she answered meekly. She prepared herself. She knew she was going to get it.

But Frank put his arm around her and said, "We were worried about you. It got dark, and your mother didn't know where you'd gone."

When they got back to the house, Michelle said, "I called Chloe's house, but she didn't know where you were. Why didn't you tell me you were leaving? You scared me half out of my mind."

"Sorry," Hallie said. She was trying to hold back tears, but she didn't have any idea why she felt like crying.

"Come on in the house now," her mother said, putting her arm around her. "It's cold."

Hallie resisted, and she and her mother hung back as Frank walked into the house.

As soon as he disappeared, Hallie started to cry.

"Get in the car," Michelle said softly. "I'll be right back."

She went into the house for a few minutes, then returned with a sweater for Hallie.

She got into the driver's side of the car and started the engine.

"Let's go get a salad," Michelle said.

"But didn't you already make dinner?" Hallie asked, surprised by her mother's suggestion.

"Dixon and Frank can eat it. We need to talk."

* * *

This time her mother listened carefully to her. She didn't make excuses for Dixon, as she usually did. She said she understood Hallie's frustration, and it was good she was talking about it.

"It's important to open up and talk about your feelings, Hallie," she said. "Sometimes people have a hard time hearing them, but if you tell them you really, really need to talk from your heart, most of the time people will at least try to listen."

"Sometimes I'm not even sure how I feel till I say it," Hallie said.

"I know," her mother agreed. "That's why it's so important to explore your feelings with someone you trust, like me or your dad."

"And listen to your body," Hallie said. She started to giggle.

"Yeah," Michelle said. She smiled at Hallie. "And don't laugh. It's true. Your mind might lie to you, but your body won't. It can't."

When they finished eating, Hallie knew they had done more than share a meal.

"Thanks, Mom," she said, giving Michelle a hug.

"I have an idea," her mother said, hugging her back. "Why don't we have a date every Friday night?"

"Just you and me?"

"Yeah. Why not?"

"Without Frank and Dixon?"

"That will give them some time together, and it will give us some time alone. It'll be fun."

"I love you, Mom."

"Want to take in a movie on our date tonight?" Michelle asked.

"Sure."

Hallie sat at her desk smiling. Maybe she should put Dixon in the plus column, as well as in the minus column. She picked up her pencil and wrote "dixon" in very small letters under the plus column.

After all, she'd gotten to see some of the movies she'd missed while she was in Oregon. And the last three Friday nights had been the best time. The best.

Chapter Twenty-two

Six o'clock. The first light of day was seeping in through the window. Hallie had never stayed up all night before. And she wasn't sure just how wide awake she was now. Maybe this was all part of a dream. Maybe she would wake up and find that Jane and Frank were merely images of her imagination, and both of her parents were asleep in the bedroom next to hers. She sighed. She knew it was no dream. She slumped down into her chair, no closer to the answer than she had been at midnight.

If only her mother would help her make a decision. If only her father would insist that she come back to Oregon. Then she could blame one of them if she made the wrong choice. But her mother said it was important for her to make the decision herself, and she had overheard her cautioning her father, when she spoke to him on the phone, not to put any pressure on Hallie. At the same time, Hallie was sure she could almost hear her mother's heart thumping loudly in her chest when she said it. She knew what her mother hoped her decision would be.

She studied the paper with Venice on top.

VENICE	
Pluses	Minuses
Hawaii	DIXON
Chloe	=====
dixon	=====
Frank	
Robert	
ballet	
MOM	

It didn't help her make her decision.

She knew it was hard for her father not to pressure her, but he had finally managed to say that whatever she decided was fine with him. Of course, she did hear Jane prompting him in the background, telling him to remind Hallie that everyone would miss her, that Molly was turning over, and that they were seriously considering getting that horse.

Well, all those things were important to Hallie. And she would sure rather spend time with Molly than with Dixon, even though things were starting to work out better between them. At least she could envision the possibility of making peace with him, thanks to her mother.

Last weekend her mother had suggested that they all go into her studio and paint together. Everyone resisted. They weren't artists. They couldn't draw a straight line. They were color-blind. But Michelle cajoled them all into it. She gave them each a large sketchbook with blank paper inside. On the outside she had printed each of their names. Then she handed out oils and tempera and told them to fill every inch of five pages. It didn't matter how they did it—with their fingers, their hands, a paint brush, mixed with water as a wash—whatever, but she said she didn't want to see one blank space on any page. "Use five colors you dislike most," she said.

"Why?" Dixon asked.

"Don't ask why. Just do it."

They all grumbled some more, but as they began squeezing out the paints, something happened, and they seemed to forget everything but the look and feel of the colors.

At first Hallie painted only with a brush. She didn't want her fingers to turn into a carnival of snake-like colors squiggling across her paper. But the brush didn't quite do it, so she smeared some pink into the corner with her index finger, then scraped out a design with her nail. She stood back and looked at it. She liked it. But she needed a wash of brown on the lower half of the page. She dipped two fingers in the paint, then began spreading it around. Pretty soon she was kneading it with the heel of her hand to get just the right look.

She was concentrating so hard, she began to sweat. She blew her bangs out of her eyes, but they kept falling down again. Finally, she reached into her pocket, pulled out a barrette and pinned back her hair. Then she really got down to business.

Suddenly, the whole afternoon was gone, and the sun was going down.

"Finish up, everyone," Michelle said. It was the first words anyone had uttered since they began.

Michelle walked over to Dixon and stood looking at

his paintings for a long time. He watched her face carefully for any sign of disapproval.

"You know what, Dixon?" she said. "I think you're very talented."

"No, n-no, I'm not," he said, stuttering slightly, the way he did sometimes when he got nervous.

"Well, I think you are," her mother insisted.

"I've never done this before in my life—except in kindergarten, maybe."

Dixon was looking down at the floor and shuffling his feet, but he couldn't quite hide the smile of gratitude that was spreading across his face.

Michelle put her arm around Dixon and gave him a squeeze, then she walked over to Frank. "And look at this," she said. "Your paintings and your father's are very similar."

She placed the two books next to each other and studied them together. They all hovered over them. Even Hallie could see the similarities.

"Wow," Dixon said, "you're right."

"I'd like to put one of your paintings up on the wall, if you don't mind, Dixon. After all, since we share this space, you ought to have something personal of yours in here, too," Michelle said.

"Could we put it above the futon?" Dixon asked.

"Sure," Michelle answered.

"Let's take a look at Hallie's," Frank said.

They walked over to where Hallie had been working. She was a little nervous having anyone stare at her art work like that, even though it was just her mother and Frank and Dixon.

"That looks like some of the drawings I saw in my social studies book," Dixon said.

"You're right, Dixon," Michelle agreed. "They look like hieroglyphics."

"It's just a design," Hallie said, feeling suddenly very shy.

"Boy, you sure got in touch with something deep inside of you," Michelle said. "The Egyptians drew these kinds of figures."

Hallie giggled softly. Maybe the Egyptians did draw these kinds of figures, and maybe she had known that on some deep, deep level. But then again, maybe she had seen them on the cover of a book jacket in a store window on Main Street when she whooshed by on her skateboard. It didn't matter, really.

Hallie was a little disappointed that her mother didn't ask if she could put one of her paintings up on the wall. But she kind of understood why she hadn't.

"Okay, gang," Frank said. "Now it's time to analyze Michelle's paintings."

Well, Michelle had worked on one oil painting on a large canvas all day. And it was horrible. Not the painting itself, but the monster she had painted. It was a dark, ugly woman that sort of looked like Michelle, but was distorted and scary.

"Is that supposed to look like you?" Frank asked.

"It is me. It's my Ereshkigal," Michelle said, "my dark side. Maybe if I paint her and acknowledge her existence inside of me more openly, she won't suddenly appear when I least expect her and ruin my day and everyone else's."

"She sure is ugly, Mom," Hallie said.

"Oh, I don't know. She's not so bad," Michelle said. "Now that I'm actually looking at her, I don't think she's so bad at all. And not nearly as scary as I thought she would be.''

They all laughed, but at the same time they all knew exactly what Michelle was saying.

"I'm starving," Frank said.

"Me too," Hallie said.

"Uh-uh," Michelle said. "Have to clean up first."

"Is that you speaking or Ereshkigal?" Frank asked.

"Both," Michelle said.

"I'll do it," Dixon said quietly.

There was a moment of stunned silence. Then everyone else said, "Great. We'll throw together some dinner."

Hallie knew that just because things had worked out that day, it didn't mean that life was always going to be easy here. She knew that she and Dixon would still fight occasionally. She still resented Frank sometimes. Not that he did anything so wrong. He was just here. That was enough. But something pretty wonderful had happened that day in her mother's studio. They had become a family. And that counted for a lot.

Six-thirty. Hallie's head slowly fell onto her desk. She closed her eyes. She turned her head a little to the side to make herself more comfortable, and her pencil dropped off the desk. She automatically reached under her desk to get it, feeling around for it with her eyes still closed. She couldn't locate it.

Finally, she opened her eyes and slid her chair back. She still couldn't see it. She crawled around on the floor. Then she finally looked under the narrow space between the bottom desk drawer and the floor. The pencil was there.

And next to it was a book.

She retrieved both of them.

She couldn't believe her eyes. She was staring at "The Country Mouse and the City Mouse."

Chapter Twenty-three

Almost in a daze, Hallie picked up the book. She sat down at her desk again and ran her hands over the cover, somehow reluctant to open the book, now that she had found it.

Finally, she took the plunge. Slowly, slowly, she began reading the children's story her mother had read to her when she was a little girl. But she couldn't keep her mind on it. She kept remembering the way she had sat, cuddled in her mother's lap, pointing to the pictures, saying the words with her. She could almost feel her mother's warm body next to hers now. She could barely tell the difference between her body and her mother's then.

She remembered feeling bereft, crying when her mother left her with a sitter so she could go to her office for a few hours to work. Then her mother would come back into the room after her nap, and they became like one body again. And Hallie was content.

But Hallie herself had broken that spell when she went to live with her father last year. She had become her own separate person. Maybe because her mother had allowed her to.

She looked down at the pages of the book again. When the city mouse went to the country, she couldn't understand how the country mouse could bear to live such a dull life where nothing ever happened. Hallie smiled. That's what she had thought when she first arrived in Oregon.

But when the country mouse went back to the city with the city mouse, there was lots of excitement. There was a banquet of exotic food left on the dinner table. The country mouse had never even seen such abundance. But before they got a chance to move cautiously across the table and grab it, a cat crept into the room and sprang up to pounce on them.

The two mice scampered away to safety, but the country mouse had had enough. She ran back home, saying she would rather live a dull life than a dangerous one.

There is all kinds of danger, Hallie thought as she looked at the picture on the last page. Maybe the most dangerous thing is not to know who you are or where you belong. Or not to let yourself know.

She closed the book and began putting it into one of the drawers, but a piece of paper fell out. She looked at it. It was a poem that her mother had written. She had glanced at it when her mother had sent it to her, but she'd never really taken the time to read it carefully. She hadn't been ready. Now she knew that she was.

upon reaching puberty: a story for my daughter

how do you feel
being new

different than you were
yesterday?
on the outside
small change.
on the inside
you know
no turning back for baby bottles
and baby talk
you loved so much not long ago
and just lately
left behind.
yet if you want to talk baby talk with me
you can do that anytime
'cause i've just met
the little girl
who lives in me
and likes to talk
baby talk
on occasion
when no two are looking
but some one who loves her
is there to listen.
you are still
my daughter
the child
in your core
in your heart
yet now
you also are
or have
or wear
another you
to walk inside,

to move, to speak, to learn
through.
take them all with you
on your journey
the past 'yous'
the present
and the 'yous' that are yet to come.
take them with you.
no need to make lonely
any one of them.

i ask you
how you felt
not expecting an answer
now.
what does it mean?
not expecting an answer
now
i do know
when i was a young girl
i misunderstood
what life was becoming.
i was not prepared
i could not blend
the beautiful
alive
child-like me
with the one
stumbling into this foreign territory
of sex
of childbirth
possibilities i did not
even

want to think about.
i deeply needed a guide
and
i had none.
i think we all
must deeply need a guide.

i ponder this moment
in all women
i ponder this moment
in myself
when i became 'woman'
and was cast in bronze
my own wax image
lost
traded for the cultural mold.
in my confusion
i accepted my fate
something less
than when i
was just a girl.
in my ignorance
i let myself swallow
an attitude
that probably
is locked
inside
my DNA.
information
bequeathed
from a time
when girls bled
and then were wed

to old men
for birthing of sons
not daughters.
in these stone age memories
i hated myself
for what i
had just turned
into.
so i ponder this moment
in you
and speak to your wholeness.

swampwoman does not know of all this
she is simple
she understands only
the beauty of change.
she can pose the question
to the inside swampwoman
and it is the question
that sheds the light
where it is dark.
the answer
not from the guide
but from the search inside.
something new about you
just born,
celebrate your health,
your femininity.
celebrate the myth and the mysteries
that television cannot give you.
celebrate what it is to be a woman.

* * *

Hallie slowly put the paper down on her desk. Tiny bubbles of excitement started forming in her stomach, and the voices deep inside her began to whisper, "Stay. Stay in Venice. Stay in California." She listened, and the voices grew louder and louder.

The tiredness began to drain out of her body.

She got up from her desk, stiff from so much sitting, and she flexed her body, slowly, slowly allowing each muscle to come alive.

The sun rose outside her window, flooding her room with light, and despite her not having slept, she was filled with energy.

She moved over to her closet and picked up her ballet slippers. The feel of the smooth, soft leather sent shivers through her, and as she quickly slipped them on her feet, her whole body, every nerve and every cell, celebrated her decision.

Her bedroom wasn't big enough to contain her feelings, so she opened her door and moved into the living room. As she pirouetted across the floor, she caught sight of her mother, still in her nightgown, standing in the doorway. She smiled at Hallie. She knew that Hallie had finally made her decision.

More wonderful novels by
MARILYN LEVY
available at bookstores everywhere.

FITTING IN

Julia Brown thought she had kissed her gorgeous Russian friend Mikhail good-bye when her vacation in Moscow was over. Then he and his family show up at the L.A. airport and it is like a dream come true. Except that Mikhail's parents can't find work and Mikhail is comfortable only with a gang of Russian hoods. Can this long-distance romance be saved?

IS THAT REALLY ME IN THE MIRROR?

Joanne Geislin has a great voice, and she's really smart. Ron and Ejaz, her only two friends, know Joanne is special but they seem to be the only ones. Joanne would do anything to be beautiful and popular like her older sister. When Joanne is in a terrible car accident and extensive plastic surgery turns her into the girl she thought she wanted to be, she learns about the danger of getting what you wish for.

THE LAST GOOD-BYE

Falling in love is the easy part. Jesse Rhomer is dark and handsome and troubled just like the heroes of the short stories Karen Mathews secretly writes. Unfortunately, Karen's dreams are about to meet the reality of involvement with someone who has had much pain and little love. Jesse wants and needs her help but he doesn't know how to ask.

MARILYN LEVY

LOVE IS NOT ENOUGH

Delphi had plans for a great summer with her new boyfriend, Nick, until she met his family. They didn't think he should date a black girl. Half African-American, half Greek, Delphi had always thought of herself as just one of the kids. Suddenly, she discovered that not everyone saw things the way she and her family did. And the people who didn't could break your heart and spirit.

NO WAY HOME

Billy Goldman had always wanted to go to Disneyland so he agreed to spend the summer with his mother in California. Since becoming a devout member of Omkara, a religious cult, she no longer drank or was depressed, so Billy thought it might be a fun way to spend his summer vacation. He didn't know he would not see anything beyond the walls of the religious commune. Where do you turn when you're a virtual prisoner of a religious cult and no one in your family seems to care?

PUTTING HEATHER TOGETHER AGAIN

Heather's new boyfriend's jealousy is sabotaging their relationship. Feeling lost and alone, Heather begins dating Joe, an older and wilder guy. Then one horrible evening, Joe refuses to take no for an answer. And Heather must find the strength to piece her life back together again.

RUMORS AND WHISPERS

Sarah Alexander hates everything about her new high school. Forced to transfer her senior year, the only bright spot in her day is art class, where her teacher encourages her and she meets a special boy. Then two issues she had never dealt with before, homosexuality and AIDS, hit close to home and make being the new girl in school the least of her problems.

MARILYN LEVY

SOUNDS OF SILENCE

Nikki is one of the beautiful people—popular, pretty, and self-assured. Then a good-looking transfer student walks into Nikki's A.P. English and into her heart. There is only one problem. Blake is deaf, and Nikki is sure her family and friends can't accept him. How long can she keep Blake a secret before she loses his love?

SUMMER SNOW

Leslie Bishop's world has been turned upside down by her parent's divorce, and she finds herself spending the summer in Los Angeles with her father. After life at home with her staid mother in Chicago, Leslie is bedazzled by life in free-wheeling L.A. When Scott, the gorgeous blond brother of a movie star, pursues her, Leslie will do anything...even cocaine...to keep him interested. She just didn't know she would get hooked.

TOUCHING

Eve Morrison loves her father, but she yearns for the time before her mother left and her father lost his job and the house smelled like beer. She learned early to take care of herself, but her father hasn't had a drink in a month, and she's met someone who looks just like Tom Cruise. Her father can't go off the wagon now. He just can't.

MARILYN LEVY